From A to ZIPPY

Getting there is all the fun.

Bill Griffith

Penguin  Books

PENGUIN BOOKS
Published by the Penguin Group
Viking Penguin, a division of Penguin Books USA Inc.,
375 Hudson Street, New York, New York 10014, U.S.A.
Penguin Books Ltd., 27 Wrights Lane,
London W8 5TZ, England
Penguin Books Australia Ltd, Ringwood,
Victoria, Australia
Penguin Books Canada Ltd, 2801 John Street,
Markham, Ontario, Canada L3R 1B4
Penguin Books (N.Z.) Ltd, 182-190 Wairau Road,
Auckland 10, New Zealand

Penguin Books Ltd, Registered Offices:
Harmondsworth, Middlesex, England

First published in Penguin Books 1991

10 9 8 7 6 5 4 3 2 1

Copyright © Bill Griffith, 1991
Introduction copyright © R. Crumb, 1991
All rights reserved.

Some of the comics in this book were first published in
newspapers, magazines and calendars.
Zippy is distributed worldwide by King Features Syndicate.

Printed in the United States of America

Designed by Bill Griffith

Thanks and a tip o' the pin to Diane Noomin, Robert Crumb,
David Stanford, Joel Goldstein, Joyce Zavarro, Becky Frazier
and Charles Bufe.

Also by Bill Griffith:
Zippy Stories
Nation of Pinheads
Pointed Behavior
Are We Having Fun Yet?
Pindemonium
King Pin
Pinhead's Progress
Get Me a Table Without Flies, Harry

"One great part of human existence
  is passed in a state which cannot
  be rendered sensible by the use of
  wideawake language, cutanddry grammar
  and goahead plot."
                    —James Joyce, 1926

CONTENTS

ZIPPY AND ME/ The Altered Ego

I've suffered three great disillusionments in my life. The first, at the age of six, came when I realized that Bob Hope didn't spontaneously spout his funny lines for the camera, but was mouthing the boffo lines others had written for him. I still laughed at "Paleface"...just not quite as loud. My second big letdown came a few years later, at the height of the Hopalong Cassidy craze, when I learned from a hipper and cooler kid that not only was William Boyd old enough to be my grandfather, but he didn't do his own stunts. It just wasn't the same anymore for this buckaroo. My third, and longest-held, illusion was dashed forever only recently when a cartoonist friend let me in on an awful truth: most New Yorker cartoonists don't write their own gags! First Bob Hope, then Hoppy and, now, Charles Addams and George Price—my heroes, tarnished, one by one. Isn't anything what it seems to be? Where will it all end?

"Dear Mr. Griffith", the letter read, "I'd like to submit jokes to your daily strip. I'm a professional gag writer." *Aaaaaargh!!* At least let me keep a few illusions about *myself* please! Whether I burn out in the next couple of years or slip gracefully into a blissful state of syndicated senility, I know one thing—no one puts words into my mouth...except Zippy.

Which brings me to my point. You see, Zippy, much like Uncle Scrooge McDuck when I was seven, is *real* to me. I don't so much write my strips (when things are going well) as wait for Zippy to tell them to me. He's there somewhere, accepting provolone into his life, as I sit staring at the pristine sheet of two-ply on my drawing board. My job is to tune him in.

Living with a non-sequitur-spouting pinhead isn't all Cool Whip and beets. Keeping in touch with that part of myself that thinks Wayne Newton is God can be a bit unnerving. If Zippy is a cross-cultural lightning rod, absorbing every sound bite and photo opportunity that comes his way, What am I? Am I Griffy, railing at a world gone mad and dressed in neon Spandex to prove it? Both Zippy and Griffy vie for attention inside my head. It's a delicate balancing act, lemme tell ya! Doing a daily strip examining the fads, foibles and fetishes of this nutty thing we like to call "western civilization" demands a character like Griffy to be the mouthpiece for my critiques. But, without Zippy, I'd just be a gloom-and-doom crank, flailing about in a sputtering rage against ugly computer graphics, smarmy televangelists and all-terrain vehicles. Zippy, for all his craziness, keeps *me* sane—and keeps Griffy from coming down with a terminal case of pessimism.

When I began drawing Zippy (in 1970), he was simply a vortex of short-circuited synapses (sound familiar?). Had he stayed that way—had he not found Griffy—he would most likely have entered the Home for Retired Cartoon Characters long ago. ("Nurse, face me sitting the Cool Whip, please...") Zippy may be me, but I'm not Zippy. I let him out—or he lets me out—as the mood (or deadline) strikes us. My function is simply to listen to what he says, "translate" it for my tiny, but highly influential, cult following, and deny all responsibility if caught with my puns down.

—Bill Griffith

INTRODUCTION by R. Crumb

MY CLOSE PERSONAL FRIEND, BILL GRIFFITH

Y'know, people always ask me, "Where do you get your material? Like, where do you get your inspiration, Bob?" (don't call me "Bob"). I have my pat come-back for this question...something "The Spain" (real name of cartoonist Manuel Rodriguez, but don't call him "Manny") once said: Man, we need an *army* of cartoonists to keep up with it!"

And here, within these pages, is the work of the most combat-hardened soldier in the whole rag-tag platoon (an army it ain't), a war-weary dogface who's seen more front-line action, who volunteers for more missions, who does more time *out there* in the horrible jungle of the modern world than any of us—than any other cartoonist in recent history that I know of. Me, I do what I think is more than my share—I put in my sweat to find the enemy and nail his ass to a piece o' Strathmore, and then I kick back, go on leave and try to forget. But I can only shake my head in amazement at *this* psycho— how does he *do* it? What demon, what Freudian subconscious childhood weirdness drives him to keep going back there, day after day? Well, my Dad was a military fanatic, same as his (see "INITIAL DEVELOPMENT", pg. 73). "It's a dirty job, but somebody has to do it." That was Bill's grim, quiet explanation, with a modest, almost apologetic shrug, when stating his motives in the documentary, "Comic Book Confidential". Well, they sure as hell aren't pinning any medals on 'im! He gets paid decently, but the glory, the adulation, goes, of course, to the *charmers*, the guys who play it *cute* for the ladies, the operators who "dumb it down" for the masses. But let's face it, Bill, they were dumb when they started! You're better off, pal!

Knowing him, though, I know it breaks his heart that they don't *get it!* (See "DAILY STRIP", pg. 7) He wants to be loved by them so *bad!* But, personally, I don't think you can have your cake and eat it too. You can't stick it to their *lifestyle* like that and then expect them to take you into their hearts. You know that, Bill, don'tchoo know that? They want to be *stroked*...they want *approval* ...they want to be patted on the back for their soft-headed, eager acceptance of cellular phones 'n' stuff. He makes a cruel mockery of Bill Cosby, nylon warm-up suits, fax machines, everything! Every teensy-tiny thing! Plastic red-and-yellow ketchup and mustard squeeze bottles! The – the mass yearning for GORE-TEX ® ! Styrofoam cups! (I have ta tell ya, Griffy, in case you haven't already heard: they now have "ozone friendly" Styrofoam cups... see "WHITE, PUFFY, LETHAL", page 54).

Myself, I can laugh my head off, because I'm an alienated crank like him...it all looks like the end o' the world to me...I, too, am "mean-spirited" 'n' filled with bile...my nervous system, too, must listen to concertina and bagpipe music to clear my brain of the killing effects of modern pop music and other electronic noise (see "ON THE CHARTS WITH A BULLET", pg. 52).

Griffith's comic strips are not sensitive enough to *their feelings* out there...he's a *wise-ass*... and then there's all those obscure references..."You gotta have a Ph.D. to understand this fershlugginer mess!" (See "TRANSLATION PROVIDED", pg. 46). Hey, Bill, that's *right!* Your strip is an endless torrent of insults flung in the face of every guy with an acrylic baseball cap. I'm surprised you haven't had the shit beat out of you yet by some '49ers fans coming out of a bar on 24th Street (his neighborhood in San Francisco is often overrun by these party dudes).

You're such a sneering, misanthropic old fuddy-duddy! Whataya, whataya *want* from them? How many of them did you expect would pick up on your snobbish art-historian take-off on Di Chirico (see "ONE FACTOID OVER THE LINE", pg. 73)? I mean, *I* got it, of course, but, you know, you gotta *sweet-talk* 'em! (See "HIS SHINING HOUR", pg. 175).

Part of Griffith's problem is he's a workaholic. Girl artist 'n' cartoonist Phoebe Gloeckner summed it up recently when she asked Bill, "Do you *ever* stop working?" He's doing a *daily strip!* It's too *common!* People don't value something they can get so easily...I'm, like, *totally* amazed that he's kept the quality up so long! I keep waiting for ZIPPY to sink into that tired-blood feeling that envelops most daily strips after a few years, if they *ever* had any life in them. Few have escaped this fate, even among the best.

Sure there's endless material, but how much can one cartoonist take? How long before Griffy busts his brisket, cut down in his prime because he was a slave to the syndicate and couldn't take a furlough? The *industrial realities* don't wait for the *muse* to get you up off your ass! That whistle blows, you *have* to fill your quota or you're *fired!* It's miraculous that he's in the daily papers at all (see "PSSSST! OVER HERE! HEY!", pg. 74), crammed in there with all that *crap*, that *drek!* I hate newspaper comics...I never read them. I find them nauseating, every one, except ZIPPY. He's a *freak* in there...he doesn't *belong*...On the other hand, the daily strip format has worked very well for him...I think the relentlessness of the daily obligation has maybe even *improved* his work, has *forced* him to comment on virtually every detail of this so-called "culture" we so-called "live" in...this - this *morass* of ridiculous nonsense, this wacky, zany...Pfffft! I sincerely hope that he can quit before he has a complete crack-up and the men in the white coats drag him away muttering, in all seriousness, "Are we having fun yet?" (see "THE FUN NEVER SETS", pg. 101) over and over and over...and over.....

R. Crumb
Winters, California
October, 1990

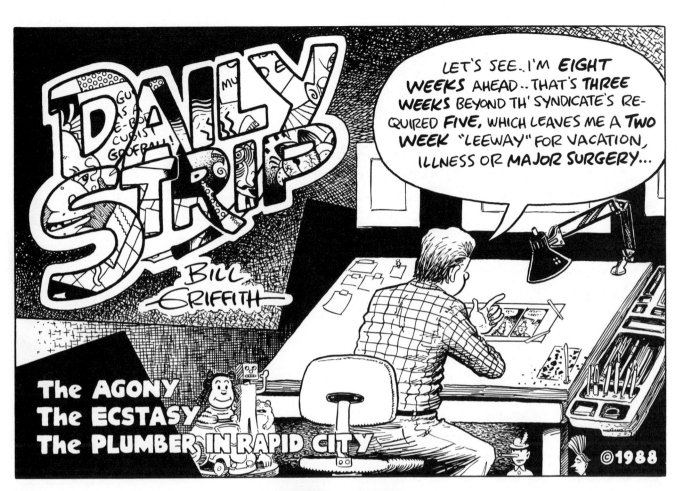

TH' MAINSTREAM.. WHY DO I FLIRT WITH IT? IT BARELY FLIRTS BACK.. SUCH IRONY.. ME..... WORKING FOR KING FEATURES..

WHAT DO THEY THINK OF MY "SENSE OF HUMOR" IN SHREVE-PORT? OR ASBURY PARK? WHAT WEIRD TWIST OF FATE LED ME TO THIS POINT?

A PINHEAD? GARRY TRUDEAU CALLS MY STUFF "ELLIPTICAL".. ..YEH..THAT'S WHAT AMERICA CRAVES..AN "EL-LIPTICAL" COMIC STRIP!!

HEY, HERRIMAN ONLY APPEAR-ED IN 45 PAPERS.. SOME NERVE.. COMPARING MYSELF TO HIM.. BUT, STILL, THERE ARE PARALLELS..

UH.. HI.. I HAVE A RESERVATION.. TH' NAME IS GRIFFITH.. RM. 204.

..GRIFFITH..YES! PLEASE FILL OUT THIS CARD.. IT'S UPSTAIRS, IN TH' REAR..A NICE CORNER ROOM..

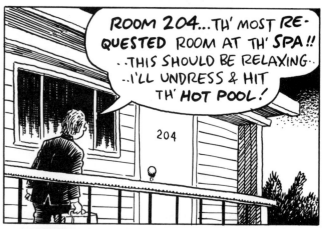

ROOM 204...TH' MOST RE-QUESTED ROOM AT TH' SPA!! ..THIS SHOULD BE RELAXING.. ..I'LL UNDRESS & HIT TH' HOT POOL!

RIGHT NOW, A PLUMBER IS READING MY STRIP IN TH' "RAPID CITY JOURNAL" & NOT GETTING IT!!

OY.. I DON'T THINK I PACKED ENOUGH BOXER SHORTS...

ZIPPY   "GOOD MORNING, CAMPERS!!"   BILL GRIFFITH

THE NEW GRIFFY DRESSES FOR A TOUGH DAY OF HEAVY CRITICAL THINKING..

I MAY LOOK A BIT ROUNDER..BUT MY MIND IS STILL HONED TO A FINE EDGE!!

I'M NEW, TOO!

Read "WEIRDO" MAGAZINE!!

OH, YEH? I GUESS IT'S A SEASON FOR CHANGE.. ..WHAT WITH A NEW PRESIDENT & A NEW CONGRESS..

I THOUGHT I WAS ELECTED PRESIDENT!

DID I TAKE A NAP AND MISS SOMETHING?

NAPPING IS OUT NOW, ZIP!! TH' REAGAN YEARS ARE OVER! WHO'S YOUR NEW ROLE MODEL?

I'M ADOPTING DAN RATHER'S CALM ASSUREDNESS TOM BROKAW'S SPEECH DEFECT..

11-16

..AND BRYANT GUMBEL'S SINCERE HANDSHAKE!!

LOVE TH' BLAZER!!

© 1988 Bill Griffith. World rights reserved. Distributed by King Features Syndicate

---

ZIPPY   "THE YOW OF KNOWING"   BILL GRIFFITH

ZIPPY, WHAT WOULD YOU SAY IF YOU WERE TOLD YOU HAD ONLY SIX WEEKS TO LIVE?

YOW!!

AND HOW WOULD YOU RESPOND TO TH' NEWS THAT YOU WERE VOTED "SEXIEST MAN ALIVE" BY COSMO MAGAZINE?

YOW!!

HOW 'BOUT IF YOU WITNESSED A VISITATION BY TH' SPIRIT BODY OF JACKIE GLEASON AT A MALL IN MIAMI BEACH?

YOW!!

11-17

"YOW"...A CRY OF PAIN, A SQUEAL OF GLEE, AN EXCLAMATION OF RELIGIOUS FERVOR...IT'S TH' ALL-PURPOSE WORD FOR EVERY SITUATION--

USE IT IN A SENTENCE TODAY!!

© 1988 Bill Griffith. World rights reserved. Distributed by King Features Syndicate

---

ZIPPY   "LOOSE VERTICAL HOLD"   BILL GRIFFITH

EVERYBODY EXPERIENCES IT SOONER OR LATER ...THAT ANNOYING SHIFT.. ..THAT UNCERTAIN FEELING ..THAT DISTURBING TRANSITION...

ARE YOU HAVING ANOTHER MID-WEST CRISIS, S.L.??

11-19

IT USUALLY COMES WHEN YOU GO FROM AN INTERIOR TO AN EXTERIOR- AN AWKWARD TEXTURAL DIFFERENCE...DO THEY THINK WE DON'T NOTICE IT??

ARE WE TALKING ARCHITECTURE OR PSYCHE, S.L.?

NEITHER, PAL..WE'RE TALKING "MASTERPIECE THEATRE"..WHEN IT GOES SUDDENLY FROM VIDEOTAPE TO FILM..LIKE WHEN SOME ARISTOCRAT LEAVES HIS MANSION TO GET IN A CAR.. I'M VISUALLY OFFENDED!

SOMETIMES IT'S COMFORTING, S.L.. JUST TO KNOW YOU'RE THERE...

© 1988 Bill Griffith. World rights reserved. Distributed by King Features Syndicate

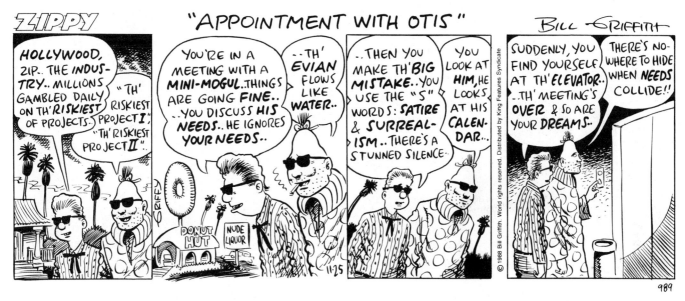

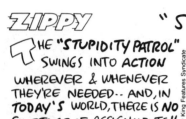

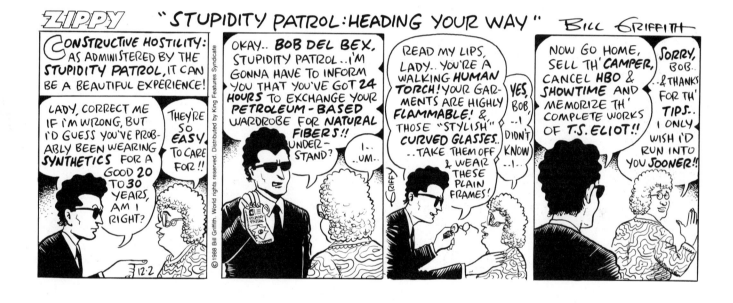

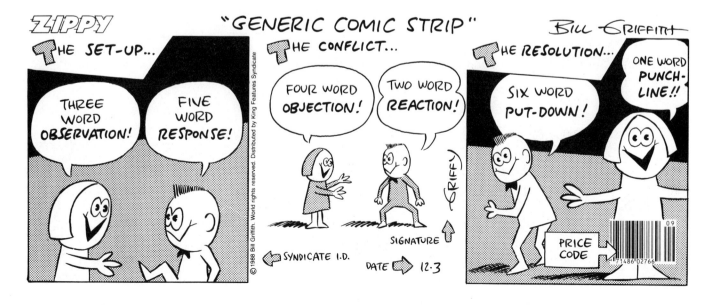

"SNOW JOKE" BILL GRIFFITH

PRETTY TH' WAY TH' LIGHTS GLOW IN ALL TH' WINDOWS...LOTS OF PARTIES AND FAMILY GATHERINGS TONIGHT..

THOUSANDS OF LITTLE JASONS AND JENNIFERS WAITING IMPATIENTLY FOR MORNING..

GRIFFY, WHO IS RUDOLPH TH' RED-NOSED REINDEER? & WHY WON'T TH' OTHER REINDEERS LET HIM PLAY IN ANY REINDEER GAMES?

CRUELTY RARELY TAKES A HOLIDAY, ZIP... HUMANS ARE AN UNFORGIVING SPECIES..

WILL PEOPLE REALLY LIVE IN PEACE SOMEDAY, LIKE ON HALLMARK GREETING CARDS?

MAYBE NEXT YEAR..

12-24

WE'RE ONLY HERE FOR A BRIEF MOMENT, ZIP..WHAT WOULD YOU LIKE FOR CHRISTMAS, ANYWAY ??

A COMPLETE SET OF "GOBOTS" AND A SUB-FREEZING WIND/CHILL FACTOR !!

© 1988 Bill Griffith. World rights reserved. Distributed by King Features Syndicate

---

 "MOE, LARRY, CURLY" BILL GRIFFITH

THE THREE STOOGES OF LIFE---

CHILDHOOD

© 1988 Bill Griffith. World rights reserved. Distributed by King Features Syndicate

MATURITY

12-26

OLD AGE

NYUK NYUK

 "OVER EASY" BILL GRIFFITH

DID I EVER TELL YOU ABOUT SALVADOR DALI'S SEX LIFE, ZIPPY ??

UH-OH...IS THIS THAT LITTLE MAN-TO-MAN TALK YOU'VE BEEN PUTTING OFF FOR 18 YEARS?

© 1988 Bill Griffith. World rights reserved. Distributed by King Features Syndicate

NOT EXACTLY.. ..ANYWAY, DALI USED TO ATTEND UPPER CRUST PARTIES WHERE HE'D MEET AND FLIRT WITH MANY HEIRESSES..

DON'T GET TOO GRAPHIC, GRIFFY.. ..I'M STILL RECOVERING FROM JESSICA RABBIT'S CLEAVAGE!

WELL, HE'D INVITE THEM UP TO HIS APARTMENT & ASK THEM TO TOTALLY DISROBE.. ..THEN, HE'D RETIRE BRIEFLY TO TH' KITCHEN & RETURN WITH TWO FRIED EGGS--

NO!!

12-27

HE'D PLACE ONE EGG ON EACH OF TH' LADY'S SHOULDERS & THEN WORDLESSLY USHER THEM OUT TH'DOOR & INTO TH' HALL-- SOME JOKER, HUH?

I'M NOT LISTENING!! SURREALISM & BREAKFAST WERE NOT MEANT TO MINGLE !!

29

1020

31

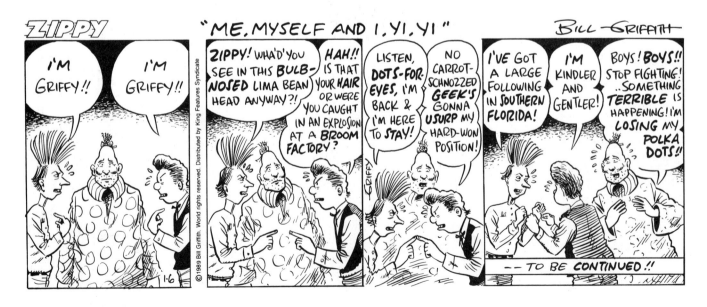

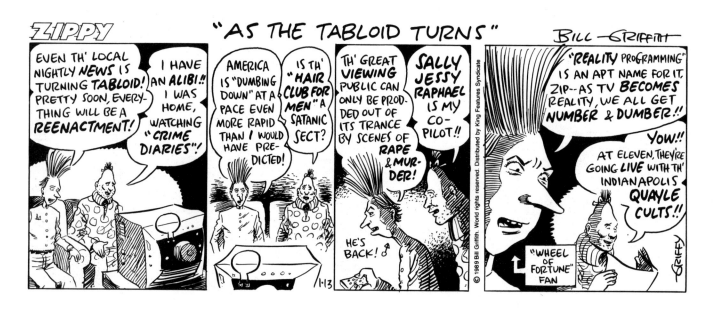

35

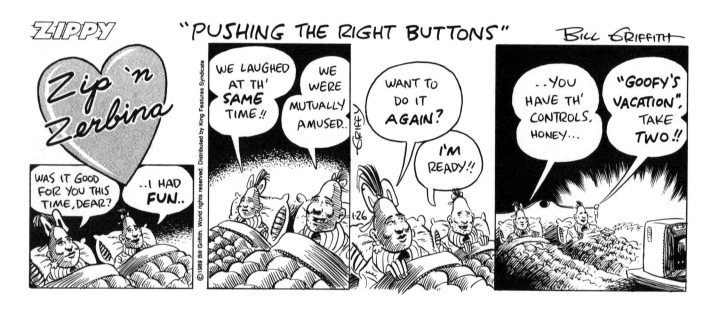

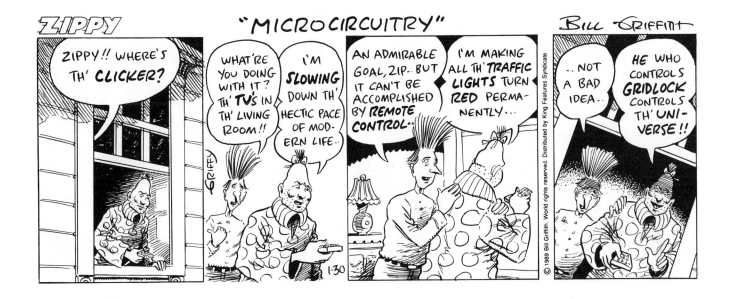

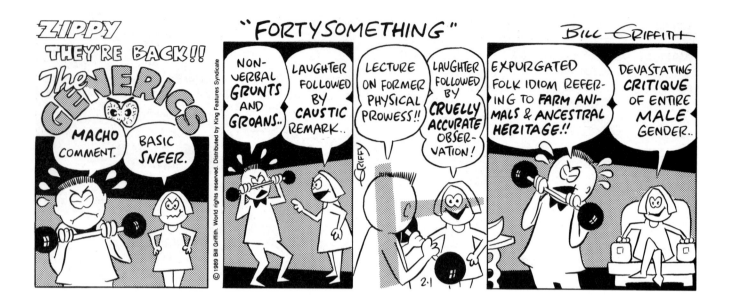

43

ZIPPY "THE EIGHTIES" BILL GRIFFITH

ZIPPY "FOREIGN OBJECTS" BILL GRIFFITH

ZIPPY "MOTOWN OR MOZART?" BILL GRIFFITH

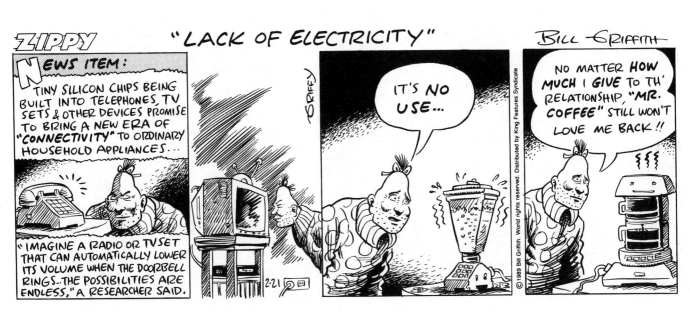

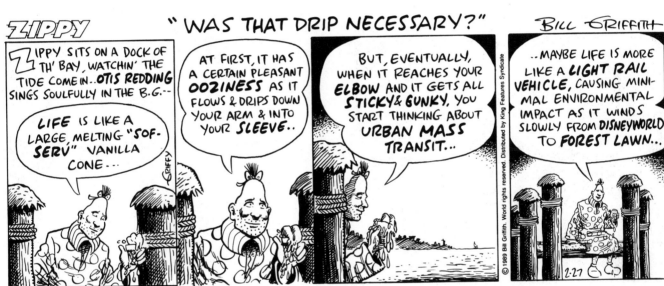

47

"URGE TO PURGE" BILL GRIFFITH

WE'VE COME A LONG WAY FROM TH' *"POWER TO THE PEOPLE"* SALUTE OF TH' SIXTIES TO TH' RAISED, LEATHER-CUFFED *FIST* OF TH' *HEAVY METAL* CONCERT.. *TEEN ANGER* TAKES MANY FORMS--

YOW!! THAT'S A *RELIEF* TO HEAR!!

WHY SO, ZIP??

I THOUGHT THEY ALL HAD TO GO TO TH' *BATHROOM* AT ONCE!!

3-14

 "JUST THE FAX, MA'AM" BILL GRIFFITH

STEP ON IT, *SHELF-LIFE!* I'VE GOTTA GET TO TH' *COPY CENTER* BEFORE FIVE!!

HEY, WHA'-D'YA GOT THERE? SIX, MAYBE SEVEN PAGES? LEMME *FAX* IT FOR YOU!!

THERE'S A FAX MACHINE AT TH' COPY CENTER.. BUT THAT WON'T SAVE ME ANY TIME--

WHAT CENTER? I GOT ONE RIGHT HERE IN TH' *CAR!* IT'S IN TH' GLOVE COMPARTMENT!

YOU'VE GOT A *FAX* IN TH' *CAR?*

SURE.. I GOT *CELLULAR* WITH CALL-WAITING, TOO!! HEY, I'M UP-TO-THE-MINUTE TECH-WISE, PAL!!

I'VE GOT INSTANT ACCESS TO *HONG KONG, JAKARTA, ATHENS*.. HEY, I'M *ON LINE,* PAL.. I'M *ON LINE!!*

WHERE'D THIS *GROCERY LIST* GET FAXED? A *SAFEWAY* IN *SINGAPORE?*

3-15

 "ART DRECKO" BILL GRIFFITH

AS A CARD-CARRYING SUPPORTER OF PUBLIC TELEVISION, THERE'S SOMETHING I'VE GOTTA SAY ABOUT THESE *"JOY OF PAINTING"* SHOWS!

DO VIEWERS OF *"MASTERPIECE THEATRE"* & *"NATURE"* REALLY WANT TO KNOW HOW TO CREATE SCHLOCK PAINTINGS OF *WATERFALLS* & *HAWAIIAN SUNSETS?*

DON'T FORGET TH' *"WET-ON-WET"* TECHNIQUE!!

I MEAN, IT'S TH' ARTISTIC EQUIVALENT OF *LEO BUSCAGLIA'S* DRIPPY *"LOVE"* LECTURES.. MY *ELITIST* SENSIBILITIES ARE ONCE AGAIN OFFENDED!

REMEMBER *DALI'S* "SAD CLOWN" PERIOD?

...JEEZ, I JUST CAN'T GET TH' *STIPPLING* RIGHT ON THIS FLORAL TRIBUTE TO *WAYNE NEWTON*..

VELVET IS A VERY DEMANDING MEDIUM!!

3-16

50

51

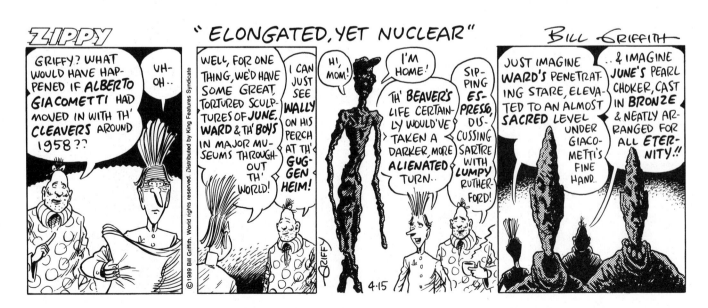

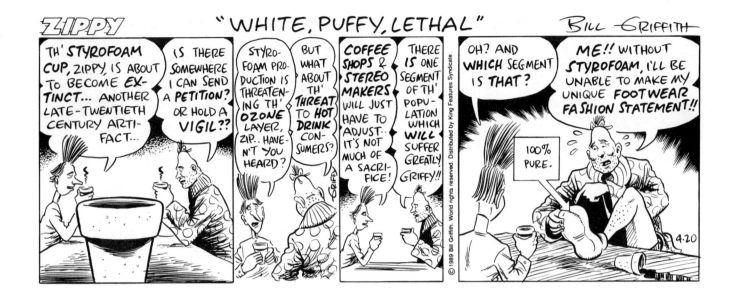

Zippy's Guide to SEX, deAth & Between-MeAl SnAcks.

55

ZIPPY
PLUGGED-IN PINHEAD

ZIPPY LIKES TO KEEP ON TOP OF ALL LATE-BREAKING NEWS..HE NEEDS TO KNOW THE COMPLETE STORY ON THAT DOWNTOWN HOSTAGE SITUATION..

I'M DEEPLY CONCERNED AND I WANT SOMETHING GOOD FOR DESSERT!!

©1982 BILL GRIFFITH

ALSO, I KNOW ALL THE DETAILS OF THAT SURGERY PERFORMED ON ENTERTAINER DOLLY PARTON!!

HEY!! DO YOU KNOW HOW THOSE MEXICAN BANK FAILURES CAN AFFECT THE PRICE YOU PAY FOR DUCT TAPE??

NOPE.

I KNOW SO MANY THINGS ABOUT SO MANY PEOPLE I'VE NEVER MET... HOW MUCH LONGER WILL CONNIE FRANCIS HAVE TO SUFFER??

IT'S EXCITING BEING A YOUNG BACHELOR ON A BUDGET, ISN'T IT, MR. TEENBEAN?

YOU TALKIN' TO ME, PAL?

NOW I'M TUCKED IN EVEN THOUGH IT'S TWO P.M. — I HOPE MY AGENT CALLS WHILE I'M ASLEEP!!

I'M PICTURING A HEAD CHEESE CASSEROLE..

IT SHOULD ARRIVE AT THE SKYWAY OFF-RAMP JUST IN TIME FOR RUSH HOUR!!

UH-OH!! IT MAY CONTAIN AN UNKNOWN SUBSTANCE!

I THINK I'LL TAKE MY VACATION IN FEBRUARY..

...HAVING A WONDERFUL TIME.. ..WISH I WAS HERE....

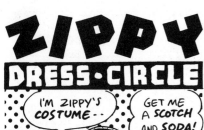

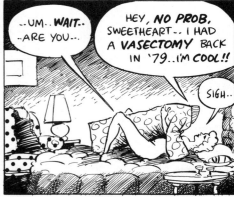

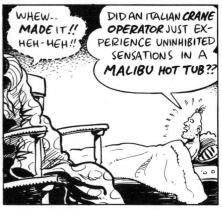

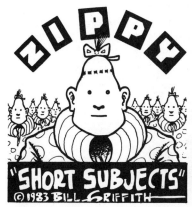

ZiPPY

"SHORT SUBJECTS"
© 1983 BILL GRIFFITH

A TRAILER PARK ON THE OUTSKIRTS OF *ISLIP*, LONG ISLAND.. *ZIPPY* AND HIS PET CAT, *DINGY*, HAVE BEEN WATCHING *HBO* FOR *39 DAYS* STRAIGHT, WHEN--

NICE *TOUPEÉ*, BURT..

DINGY, I THINK WE'RE ABOUT TO REAPPEAR IN AN OUT-OF-STATE AUTO SEAT-COVER SHOWROOM!!

I *KNEW* THIS WOULD HAPPEN!!

YEH, I'M CLOSIN' UP SHOP AFTER SEVEN YEARS - IN *TODAY'S WORLD*, WHAT ELSE COULD I DO??

..ENTER A CAREER IN *BROADCASTING*?

Z IPPY WAS RIGHT. *EXCESSIVE VIEWING* HAD CAUSED A REALIGNMENT OF HIS ORTHOMOLECULAR STRUCTURE--

MAYBE I SHOULD'VE OPENED THAT *SHAKEY'S* OUT ON ROUTE 17..

IT'S *TOO LATE* FOR THAT KIND OF TALK *NOW*, BURT !!

PURR..

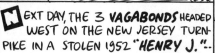

N EXT DAY, THE 3 *VAGABONDS* HEADED WEST ON THE NEW JERSEY TURNPIKE IN A STOLEN 1952 *"HENRY J."*--

IT'S JUST LIKE WITH *LIBERACE*.. YOU GO ALONG ALL YOUR LIFE.. THEN, ALL OF A SUDDEN - *BOOM!*

MENTALLY, I'VE LIVED WITH *LIBERACE* SINCE 1975 !!

HEY, THAT TUNNEL AHEAD ISN'T ON TH' *MAP!*

I'M SCARED. I'M HUNGRY. I'M COMPUTER GENERATED.. I'M *WAYNE NEWTON!*

S OMEWHERE IN THE *UTAH* DESERT, THE LITTLE VEHICLE TOOK A *DETOUR* AND PICKED UP THE SPIRIT-BODY OF THE POPULAR ENTERTAINER ...

ALL RIGHT, YOU *JERKS!* WE'LL BE IN *VEGAS* BY TONIGHT & YOU'RE GONNA BE MY BACK-UP VOCALISTS!! ...THERE'S *SHEET MUSIC* IN THE GLOVE COMPARTMENT- START *REHEARSIN'*!!

BUT, WAYNE- WHERE DO YOU KEEP THE *LINGERIE*?

DO WHAT I SAY OR YOU'LL NEVER GET BACK!

T HE THREESOME HAD STUMBLED INTO A *TIME TUNNEL* & WERE STUCK IN *JUNE, 1957* !!

W AYNE'S BRAVADO TURNED TO ANXIETY AS THE GAMBLING MECCA NEARED.. SUDDENLY, HE BEGAN SPOUTING *GUTTERAL GERMAN*--

SCHLECHTER STUHLGANG ALLEIN IST *NICHT* FÜR EINE GRÖSSENE MISSERANTE *VELANT-WORTLICH !*

I UNDERSTAND A *LITTLE* -- HE SAYS HE WANTS "FOUR DOZEN *FUZZY DICE*"!!

IS THIS ANOTHER SEQUEL TO *SMOKEY* & TH' *BANDIT?*

LAS VEGAS 7 MILES

GALLENSTEINE UND BUTTERMILCH !!

T HEY WERE *TRAPPED* - UNABLE TO RETURN TO ISLIP... AND *BURT REYNOLDS* WAS STILL A TEEN-AGER LIVING IN AMARILLO, TEXAS..

J UST AS THINGS WERE AT THEIR BLEAKEST, ZIPPY SPOTTED A *FOTO-BOOTH* & PULLED DINGY & THE SALESMAN IN WITH HIM--

THIS *MUST* BE 1983!! ---I'M *UNEMPLOYED!*

INSERT 50¢

ADJUST SEAT

I T WAS AN *AIR VENT* OF THE UTAH *TIME TUNNEL* !!

M EANWHILE BACK IN 1957--

AUF WIEDERSEHEN.. AUF WIEDERSEHEN!!

--SUCH A *NICE* SENTIMENT !! ..I'LL TAKE TWO..

I RONICALLY, NEWTON'S LAMENT TURNED OUT TO BE THE BASIS FOR HIS FIRST MAJOR *HIT*, PAVING THE WAY TO A FINANCIAL *EMPIRE* THAT WOULD EVENTUALLY LAND HIM ON THE *HOT SEAT* WITH THE NEVADA GAMING COMMISSION !!

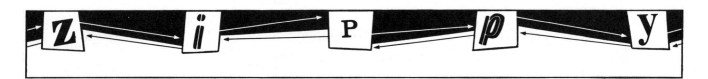

ZIPPY "LIFE WITHOUT RETAIL" BILL GRIFFITH

I HEARD IT ON **DONAHUE** TODAY, ZIP... JUST AN HOUR AGO..

THEN IT **MUST** BE TRUE..

TH' **WORLD'S** GONNA **END** FRIDAY, SEPTEMBER FIRST...

KINDA MAKES YOU **CHERISH** TH' FEW THINGS YOU **STILL** HAVE..

YEH, LIKE **WHAT?**

ONE HUNDRED AND EIGHTEEN **SHOPPING** DAYS...

ZIPPY "THE 21ST CENTURY BLUES" BILL GRIFFITH

WHAT ABOUT THIS **DRIFT** TO TH' **RIGHT,** MORALITY-WISE, ZIPSTER?

JUST SAY NO TO **SNOW** WHITE'S KNEES..

THINGS GET **CRAZIER** AS WE APPROACH TH' **MILLENIUM!!**

I WAS GIVEN A **MILLENIUM** ONCE.. IT WAS VERY **UNCOMFORTABLE..**

UH-OH.. I THINK I JUST HAD AN **IMPURE** CONCEPT!!

I WON'T TELL **PROCTOR & GAMBLE** IF YOU WON'T...

ZIPPY "CONTROVERSY" BILL GRIFFITH

PEOPLE..

HOW YOU GONNA FIGURE 'EM?

DON'T BOTHER, S.L.-- JUST STAND BACK AND ENJOY THE **EVOLUTIONARY** PROCESS..

ZIPPY — "BUILDING TO A POINT" — BILL GRIFFITH

TH' GREY AREAS ARE RAPIDLY DISAPPEARING, ZIPSTER..

BACKGROUND & FOREGROUND ARE GRINDING TO A HALT..

5-11

BUT THINGS CAN'T ALWAYS BE SEEN IN TERMS OF BLACK AND WHITE..

MY OPINIONS ARE COLORED..

WHEN YOU TAKE A HARD LINE YOU TRAP YOURSELF IN A BOX..

NOT ME! I CAN'T CONTAIN MY THOUGHTS!!

ZIPPY — "PEDS FROM SPACE" — BILL GRIFFITH

ALL THOSE THOUSANDS OF HABITABLE PLANETS OUT THERE, ZIP..

MANY WITHOUT SIGOURNEY WEAVER!!

ONE OF 'EM'S GOTTA HAVE WEIRD, ALIEN LIFE FORMS!!

IT DOES! I'VE ALREADY MET SEVERAL IN SCHOOL CROSSINGS & HOSPITAL ZONES!

5-12

THINK OF TH' MARKETING POTENTIAL..

WE ARE NOT ALONE...

ZIPPY — "WINDOW OF OPPORTUNITY" — BILL GRIFFITH

IT'S SCARY.. I'M BEGINNING TO LIKE THIS FEELING OF "SPLENDID ISOLATION"...

QUICK! DO 5 MINUTES OF HOME SHOPPING!!

CAPADIMONTE CLOWNS.. GOLD CHAINS.. PORCELAIN COLLECTIBLES..

THAT'S RIGHT.. ABSORB TH' HEALING ENERGY!!

THANKS, PAL! FOR A WHILE THERE, I THOUGHT I'D NEVER INTERACT WITH MY FELLOW HUMANS AGAIN..

OPERATORS ARE ALWAYS STANDING BY---

5-13

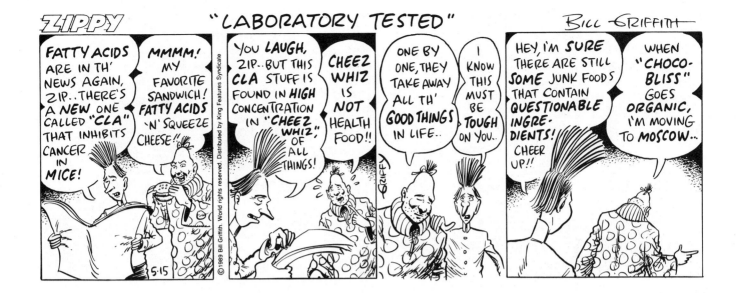

71

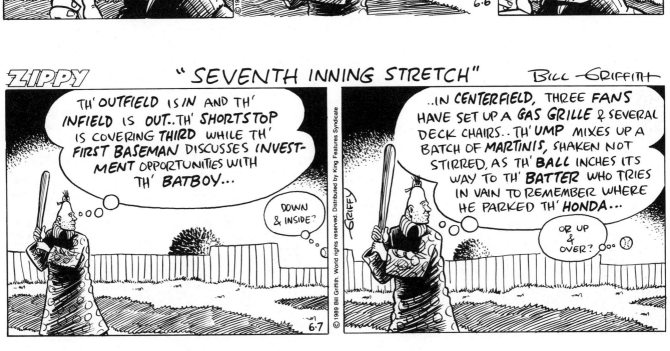

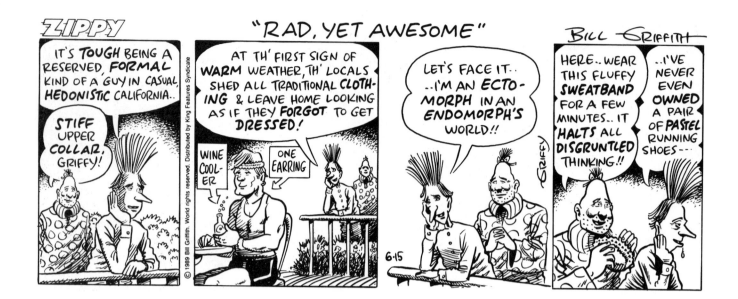

"HUMONKEY BUSINESS"

 "LOOK AT ME I'M WALKING" BILL GRIFFITH

ZIPPY **"THE JERRYNESS OF IT ALL"** BILL GRIFFITH

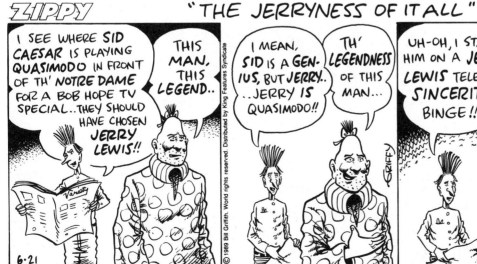

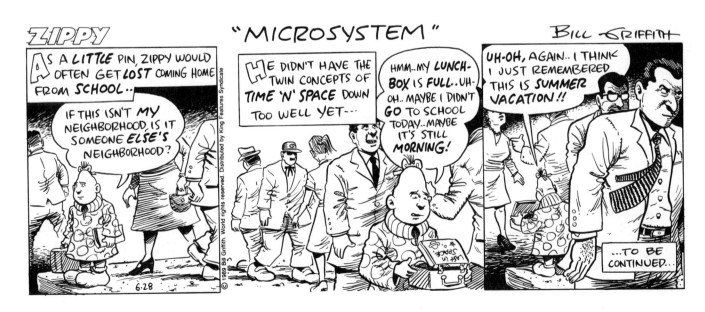

ZIPPY — "MEDIUM EVENT" — Bill Griffith

I'M LOST..BUT MY LUNCHBOX CONTAINS ALL SEVEN MAJOR FOOD GROUPS!

IF I HOLD THIS BOTTLE OF TACO SAUCE AGAINST MY CHEEK AND QUIETLY MUNCH MY DING-DONG, PERHAPS 7 OR 8 KIDS WILL ASK ME TO PLAY PARCHEESI..

6-29

IT'S GETTING LATE.. MAYBE I SHOULD DO SOMETHING TO ATTRACT ATTENTION!

AM I ON TH' EVENING NEWS YET??

© 1989 Bill Griffith. World rights reserved. Distributed by King Features Syndicate

---

ZIPPY — "CONDENSED" — Bill Griffith

LITTLE ZIPPY IS LOST..HE DOESN'T YET UNDERSTAND THE TWIN CONCEPTS OF ROAD MAPS & CHILDHOOD..

IF I SIT HERE LONG ENOUGH, WALTER CRONKITE WILL NOTICE ME, I'LL BE FAMOUS & THEN I CAN GO HOME!

HELLO, LITTLE BOY!

THE YEAR IS 1961..

YOU'RE NOT WALTER CRONKITE!! ..I NEED MEDIA ATTENTION!

YOU'RE WEIRD..

I'M HAVING A VISION--- ELIZABETH TAYLOR IS A FRAGRANCE.. ..SOPHIA LOREN IS SELLING EYEWEAR..

VERY WEIRD..

6-30

SOMEWHERE ON MADISON AVENUE, ANDY WARHOL IS STARING AT A CAMPBELL'S SOUP CAN!!

VERY VERY WEIRD...

© 1989 Bill Griffith. World rights reserved. Distributed by King Features Syndicate

---

ZIPPY — "KIDULTS" — Bill Griffith

I'L ZIPPY'S ENTIRE CHILDHOOD'S FLASHING BEFORE HIS EYES..

YO, BRO!! WHAT'S HAPPENIN'? YOU COMIN' HOME FOR LUNCH?

I WAS INSTRUCTED BY SOPHIA LOREN TO STAY ON THIS CORNER UNTIL I BECOME EITHER FAMOUS OR A FRAGRANCE..

7-1

HEY, ADULTS ARE BAD NEWS, ZIP! I TOOK A VOW! I'M NEVER GONNA GROW UP!!

ETERNALLY SHORT.

TH' WAY I FIGURE IT, WHEN YOU GET BIG, YOU JUST GET BIGGER PROBLEMS!

FOREVER SQUAT!!

HEY, IT'S TH' TOAD! HOW'S LIFE IN TH' MANIC DEPRESSIVE LANE, AMPHIBIOUS ONE?

LIPPY!! MY MAN! YOU WANNA BUY A PREVIOUSLY OWNED MOUNDS BAR??

© 1989 Bill Griffith. World rights reserved. Distributed by King Features Syndicate

84

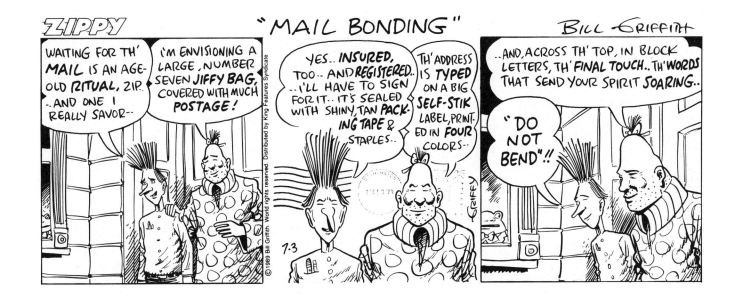

86

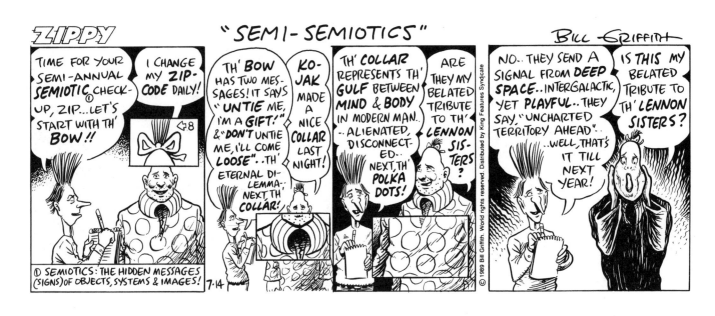

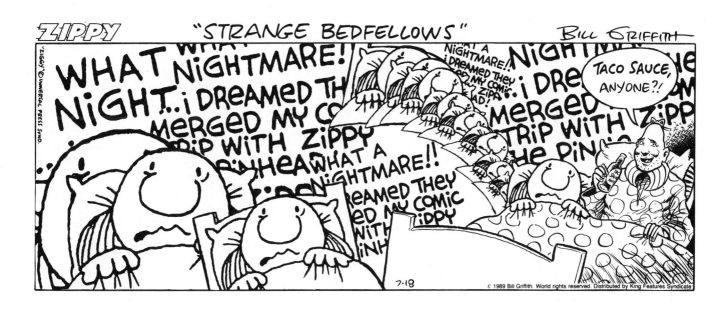

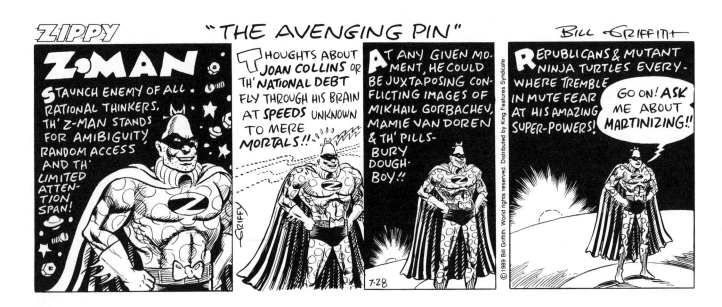

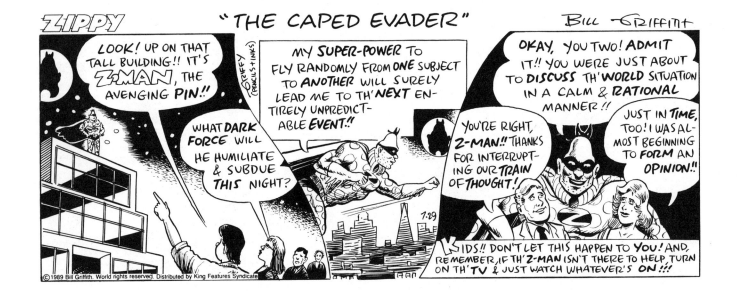

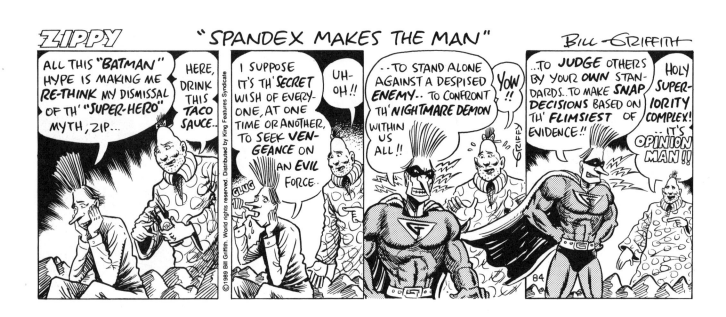

94

ZIPPY — "THE GRAPHIC EQUALIZER" — BILL GRIFFITH

IT WAS A *SIMPLE* CASE. FIND THE *GIRL*, RETURN HER TO THE BOSOM OF HER FAMILY & KEEP THE *COPS* OUT OF IT..

BUT HE HADN'T COUNTED ON THE DAPPER LITTLE MAN WITH THE CHEAP TOUPEÉ.. OR THE *SAP* FROM BEHIND THAT SENT HIM TUMBLING INTO A BIG, BLACK, INKY *VOID*...

WHY DID IT ALWAYS *END* LIKE THIS? ALONE IN A HOSPITAL BED, AN OUT-OF-FOCUS *DANA ANDREWS* TRYING TO SELL HIM *STEREO* COMPONENTS?

I DON'T KNOW.. ..HI-SPEED *DUBBING?* ..OR A *DIGITAL* CONVERTER? I DON'T KNOW.. I *DON'T KNOW!!!*

8-7

ZIPPY — "LIMITED LIFETIME WARRANTY" — BILL GRIFFITH

OF *COURSE* SHE WAS BEAUTIFUL...AND *TOUGH*.. THE ONES WHO WITHHELD CRUCIAL *INFORMATION* USUALLY WERE..

SURE SHE WAS A *CHISELER*..BUT SHE WAS *HIS* CHISELER..AT LEAST HE THOUGHT SO.. RIGHT UP UNTIL SHE DOUBLE-CROSSED HIM BEHIND THE "CLOUDLAND *CYCLONE*"!

WHY DID IT ALWAYS *END* LIKE THIS? HALF-CONSCIOUS IN THE ARMS OF *MARGUERITE CHAPMAN*, AS SHE TRIES TO SELL HIM A *LA-Z-BOY*® "RECLINA-ROCKER", BELOW MANUFACTURER'S *LIST?*

3-WAY FOOT-REST? SIMULATED *OAK* TRIM? ..I DON'T *KNOW*.. ..I *DON'T KNOW!!!*

8-8

ZIPPY — "THE BIG CHILL-OUT" — BILL GRIFFITH

GUNS. IN HIS BUSINESS, EVERYBODY'S GOT 'EM.. ESPECIALLY THE WALDOS ON THE *WRONG* SIDE OF THE LAW WHO LIKE THE WAY THEY GO *BANG* & MAKE BIG, ROUND *HOLES* IN YOUR DESIGNER *MUU-MUU*...

HE WAS *GOOD* IN A FIREFIGHT..TWO YEARS IN 'NAM *MADE* YOU GOOD..BUT, JUST LIKE 'NAM, IT WASN'T SO EASY TO TELL THE *GOOD* GUYS FROM THE *BAD* GUYS..

8-9

WHY DID IT ALWAYS *END* LIKE THIS? ..WITH *WARREN HYMER* AT THE OTHER END OF THE BARREL, UNABLE TO DECIDE IF HE REALLY NEEDED A 21 CUBIC FEET, FROST-FREE *AMANA?*

TH' SEE-THRU *MEAT KEEPER* OR TH' ADJUSTABLE DEEP DOOR SHELVES..I DON'T KNOW.. I *DON'T KNOW!!!*

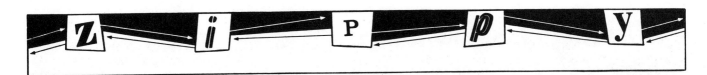

ZIPPY

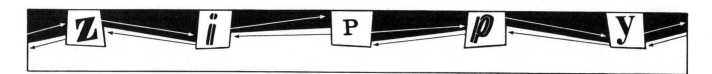

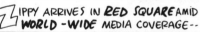

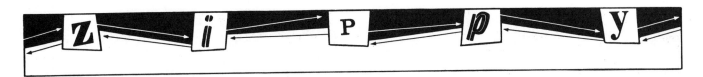

ZIPPY'S PRESIDENTIAL **EFFORT** IS OFF TO AN EXCITING START. HE'S MENTALLY WON SEVERAL KEY NOMINATIONS & IMAGINES HIS SUPPORT TO BE BROAD-BASED. THE 'YUPPY' VOTE IS STAYING AWAY IN DROVES BUT ZIPPY SAYS THIS WAS "PRE-PLANNED & 100% NATURAL."

WHAT'S THE HUBBUB? A PRESS CONFERENCE?

MUST BE FRITZ OR RONNIE..

IF ELECTED, I PROMISE TO CONVERT TO AN IRRESPONSIBLE MOSLEM SUB-SECT!!

AND, AS CHIEF EXECUTIVE, I WILL ACCEPT MY OWN **RESIGNATION** AT TH' SLIGHTEST HINT OF WRONG-DOING.... I'LL EVEN RESIGN BEFORE NOV. 6TH IF PROVOKED!!

WAIT A MINUTE!! I JUST RE-PHRASED MY NEW CAMPAIGN SLOGAN—"LET'S STAY IN BED UNTIL 1999!!"

AS ZIPPY'S PRESIDENTIAL ART DIRECTOR, I'M PLEASED TO ANNOUNCE THAT TH' FIRST DEBATE IS SCHEDULED FOR NEXT MONDAY!

THE BIG DAY..

..LADIES & GENTLEMEN- IN KEEPING WITH THE REQUEST OF THE LEAGUE OF WOMEN VOTERS AND THE VAST MAJORITY OF THE AMERICAN PEOPLE, THE FIRST PART OF THIS CONFRONTATION AMONG THE LEADING PRESIDENTIAL CONTENDERS WILL BE HELD IN COMPLETE SILENCE...

OFFICIAL MODERATOR

OKAY, CANDIDATES, PRESENT YOUR IMAGES---

BORAK
REPUBLICAN

IDAHO'S FINEST INSTANT
DEMOCRAT

PINDEPENDENT

NEXT, EACH CANDIDATE WILL GIVE HIMSELF A QUICK, PUNCHY MINI-REVIEW!!

WELL...

OFFICIAL MODERATOR

1.
"AN OSCAR-WINNING PERFORMANCE AT LAST!! SHOULD BE GOOD FOR AT LEAST ONE BLOCKBUSTER SEQUEL!!"

©1984 BILL GRIFFITH
REM

2.
"CARING, COMPASSIONATE, WHITE & FLUFFY — A LOW-DEFINITION FILLER, ASSUMES ALMOST ANY SHAPE!!"

MNM.. SOFT.. WARM..

MR. MUSHY
DEMOCRAT

3.
"... TAPERED, HALF-COCKED, ILL-CONCEIVED AND TOTALLY TAX-DEFERRED! ..THIS YEAR'S CONSUMER FAD!!"

BANANA OIL

INDEPENDENT

SOMEWHERE NEAR KANSAS-

THIS IS SOME COUNTRY, ISN'T IT, ALICE??

LET'S GO OUT & SIMONIZE THE MISSILE, MERV!!

NEXT: ZIPPY GOES INSANE!!

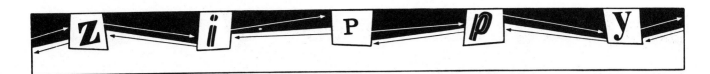

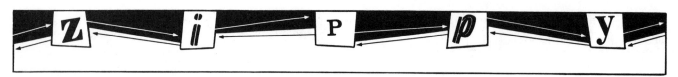

Zippy
AM I RE-ELECTED YET?
ZIPPY CAMPAIGN '84
THE UNAUTHORIZED VERSION
REAGAN CAMPAIGN HEADQUARTERS, THREE DAYS BEFORE THE ELECTION..
THE LATEST SURVEY SHOWS BONZ..UH..TH' PRESIDENT LEADING BY ONLY 3 POINTS!
HOW'S THAT NEW TV SPOT COMING?
YOU JUST SAW IT, MUFFY.. YOU AND 120 MILLION OTHER LOYAL, WHITE, GOD-FEARING VIEWERS--
YOU MEAN..
YES, WE'RE LAUNCHING A 48-HOUR SUBLIMINAL VIDEO BLITZ!!
© 1984 BILL GRIFFITH
HERE, I'LL FREEZE THAT FRAME.. IT LASTS A FIFTH OF A SECOND.. JUST LONG ENOUGH TO ANCHOR DEEP INTO THE SPONGE-LIKE SUBCONSCIOUS MIND OF THE AVERAGE AMERICAN VOTER!!
"HE'S FUN AND FRIENDLY".. ..BRILLIANT!!
CLIK!
HE'S FUN AND FRIENDLY!
MEANWHILE, AT "ZIP-CENTRAL", HIGH IN THE HOLLYWOOD HILLS--
WHAT DO YOU THINK? WE CAN HAVE 25 MILL PRINTED BY TOMORROW!!
IT'S PERFECTO! LET'S GET THESE PLASTERED ON EVERY ABANDONED BLDG. FROM HERE TO TH' BRONX!
ZIPPY
HE'S FRIENDLY AND FUN!
SHELF-LIFE, CAN WE DUMP RONNIE BUT KEEP NANCY? SHE JUST CAME OUT AGAINST VALIUM!
SURE.. HEY, WHAT ABOUT THIS SLOGAN IN '88? "FOUR MORE BEERS!"..
CAN I HAVE A TRIVIAL FUR SUIT?
SOON..
FUN 'N FRIENDLY.. FUN 'N FRIENDLY.. FUN 'N FRIENDLY..
FRIENDLY 'N FUN.. FRIENDLY 'N FUN.. FRIENDLY 'N FUN....
HE'S FRIENDLY AND FUN!
FUN 'N FRIENDLY.. FUN 'N FRIENDLY.. FUN 'N FRIENDLY..
FRIENDLY 'N FUN... FRIENDLY 'N FUN. FRIENDLY 'N FUN...
FUN 'N FRIENDLY FUN 'N FRIENDLY FUN 'N F
ELECTION DAY--
..FUN 'N FRIENDLY 'N FRIENDLY 'N FUN 'N FUNDLY 'N FRIEND 'N...
WE HAVE A WINNER! ALL THREE NETWORKS ARE CALLING IT A VICTORY FOR THE FORMER NOUGAT MIXER FROM TOLEDO!!
HOW DOES IT FEEL ZIPPY? YOU'RE NOW PRESIDENT OF THE UNITED STATES OF AMERICA!!
YOW!
... CAN I MAKE FUN 'N FRIENDLY, OFF TH' RECORD REMARKS THAT THREATEN THE STABILITY OF EAST-WEST TENSIONS YET??
NEXT: LIFE IN THE AWFUL OFFICE!!

ZIPPY THE PINHEAD

ZIPPY GOES SHOPPING FOR SUPPER AND RETURNS WITH 37 DEFECTIVE FLASH CUBES, A PLASTIC SAXOPHONE AND A SUBSCRIPTION TO "BOY'S LIFE."

I PURCHASE WHATEVER THEY TELL ME TO ON UHF-TV!!

COME ON DOWN!

GLICK!

ZIPPY REMAINS ON ONE STREETCORNER FOR 3 DAYS WAITING FOR THE "PED CROSSING"..

HI, GUYS 'N' GALS!!

PED CROSSING

NEXT, ZIPPY OFFERS SAGE ADVICE TO THE DOOR-MAN OF A FANCY PARK AVENUE APARTMENT BUILDING...

WORLD WAR III CAN BE AVERTED BY AD-HERENCE TO A STRICT DRESS CODE!!

ON LINE WAITING TO SEE "SUPERMAN II" A MEAN PERSON TELLS ZIPPY HE WILL EVENTUALLY GROW OLD AND DIE...

DOES THAT MEAN I CAN GO OFF MY DIET??

ONE WAY

LOADING ZONE

ZIPPY BELIEVES HE IS PLAYING SCRABBLE WITH DORIS DAY AND WALTER CRONKITE. JUST THEN, FRANKIE AVALON ARRIVES & BURSTS INTO TEARS..

WANNNH!! WANNNH!!

IN LATVIA, THEY HAVE A NAME FOR THIS CONDITION!!

FINALLY, ZIPPY REMEMBERS HE WAS ONCE A DRUGGIST IN KANSAS CITY IN 1952...

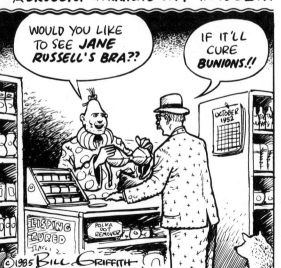

WOULD YOU LIKE TO SEE JANE RUSSELL'S BRA??

IF IT'LL CURE BUNIONS!!

OCTOBER 1952

LISPING CURED HERE

POLKA DOT REMOVER

© 1985 BILL GRIFFITH

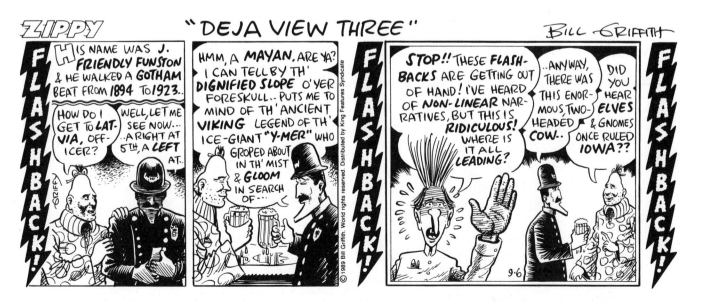

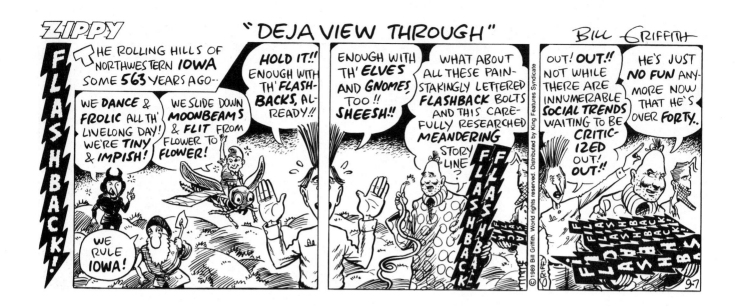

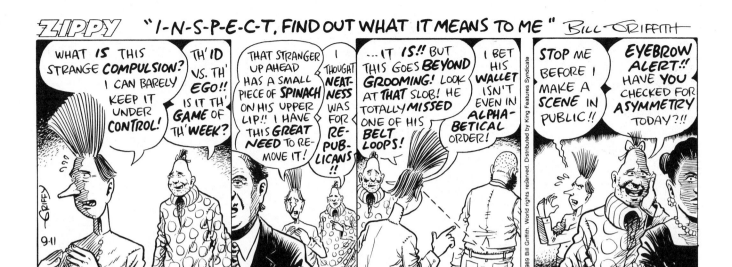

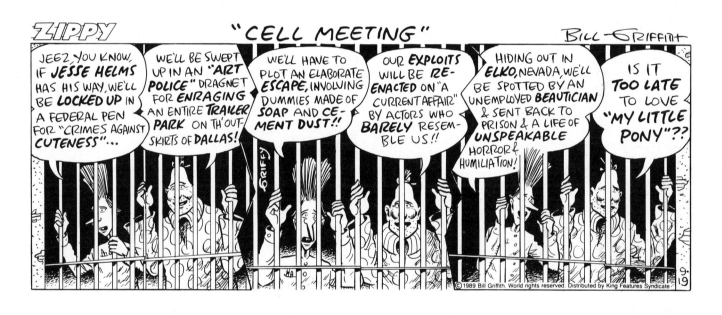

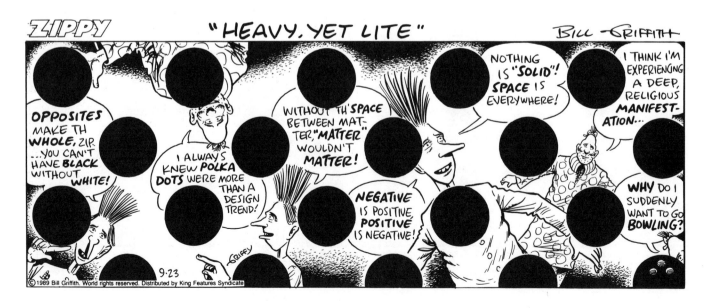

ZIPPY

"LAUNDRY: THE FIFTH DIMENSION"

BILL GRIFFITH

ZIPPY & GRIFFY ARE ABSORBED IN THEIR NEW TOYS--"VIRTUAL REALITY" SIMULATORS... TH' BOYS ARE ENJOYING WILD, SENSORY EXPERIENCES WITHOUT EVER LEAVING THEIR PATIO!

YOW!

THIS IS GREAT! I'M FLY-ING!! TH' SENSATION IS SO PHYSICAL! THIS IS AMAZING!

TH' MINI-TV'S IN THESE GOGGLES REALLY MAKE YOU BELIEVE YOU'RE THERE! WHOA! I'M SOARING THROUGH TH' GRAND CANYON!

YOW!

NOW I'M AT TH' CONTROLS OF A SPACESHIP CIRCLING SATURN! I'M WHIPPING PAST TH' RINGS & DOWN TO TH' SURFACE! WHOOO-EEE!! THIS IS FUN!

YOW!

WHAT IMPOSSIBLY EXOTIC, YET SENSUOUS, PHYSICAL SEN-SATIONS ARE YOU CHOOSING TO SIMULATE, ZIPPY??

DON'T EVER MAKE ME LEAVE THIS CLOTHES DRYER!!!

9-28

ZIPPY

"BAN THE BELLY BAG!!"

BILL GRIFFITH

SHOULDER PADS! TANK TOP CUT-OFFS! UNDER-WEAR ON TH' OUTSIDE!! AND NOW THIS!!

SHELF-LIFE! TALK TO ME! WHAT'S TH' FUSS? WHY TH' BROU-HAHA?

YECH

..THEY STARTED AS "FANNY PACKS" FOR HIKERS, BUT NOW THEY'RE EVERYWHERE! I'M RE-PULSED!!

HMM-- ..AS USUAL, S.L.'S ON TH' CUT-TING EDGE OF FASHION OUT-RAGE!

9-29

THERE'S ONE!! THEY HANG OUT OVER TH' ABDOMEN LIKE SOME GORE-TEX APPENDAGE! HEY, LADY!!

GOOD LORD! S.L.'S RIGHT! AES-THETIC ALERT! AESTHETIC ALERT!

E.U.

MAKE MY DECADE! TAKE THAT THING OFF & RE-JOIN TH' FOOD CHAIN!!

IT'S A GOOD THING WE'RE CARTOON CHARACTERS! OTHERWISE, WE'D GET WHUPPED UPSIDE TH' HAID!!

ZIPPY

"OFF THE BACK BURNER"

BILL GRIFFITH

I'VE GOT A NEW THEORY, ZIPPY... CON-CERNING TH' POP-ULARITY OF ALUMINUM & CULTURAL MEMORY LOSS..

I CAN'T REMEM-BER-- ARE WE HAVING TH' SNOUT N' KNUCKLE CASSEROLE" OR TH' "BAKED BEAN SUR-PRISE"?

9-30

ALUMINUM IS IN CONSTANT CONTACT WITH OUR FOOD, ZIPPY! -- & IT'S BEEN PROVEN TO HAVE A DETRIMENTAL EFFECT ON TH' MIND!

I ALWAYS KNEW TH' BRAIN PAN & TH' FRY-ING PAN WERE ONE & TH' SAME!

ALUMINUM IS A MAJOR INGRED-IENT IN DEODOR-ANT, &, OF COURSE, THERE'S ALUMINUM FOIL!!

...TH' MAJOR INGREDIENT IN DC-10'S!

ALUMINUM MAKES US FORGET, ZIPPY--AND A WORLD THAT FORGETS ITS OWN PAST IS DOOMED TO REPEAT IT!!

WE COULD ALWAYS SEND OUT TO TH' 19TH CEN-TURY FOR "EGGPLANT MEDLEY"!!

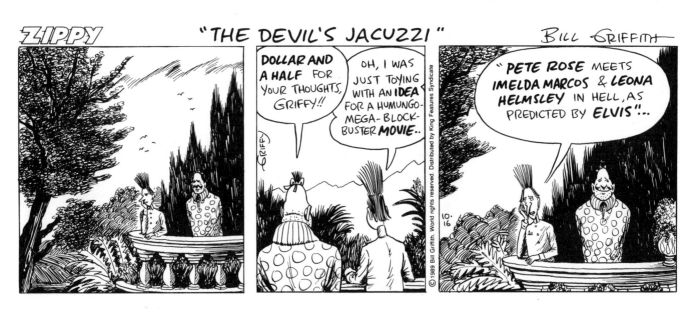

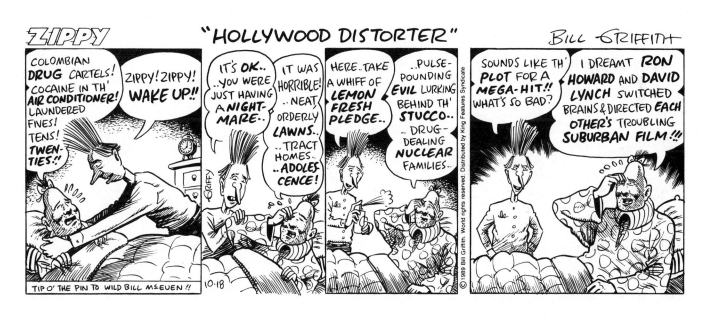

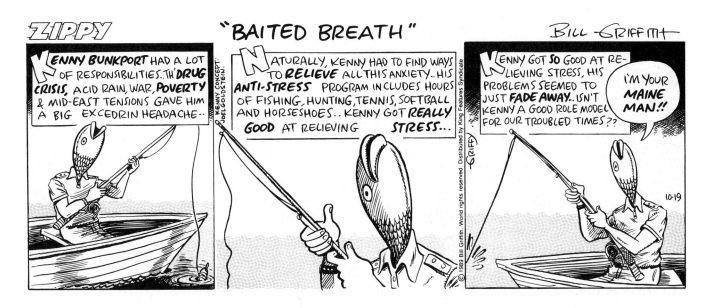

ZIPPY   "WHEN LIFESTYES COLLIDE"   BILL GRIFFITH

ZIPPY   "SAVE CAP'N CRUNCH"   BILL GRIFFITH

ZIPPY   "WAR IS PEACE"   BILL GRIFFITH

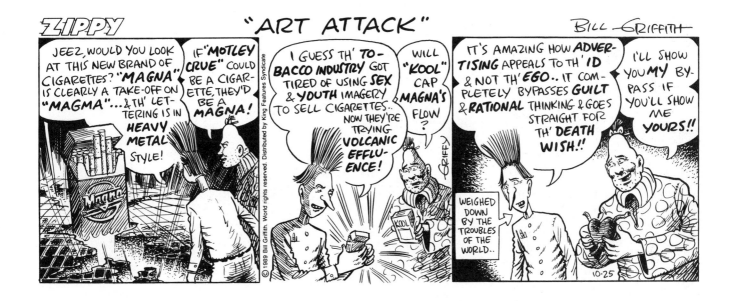

129

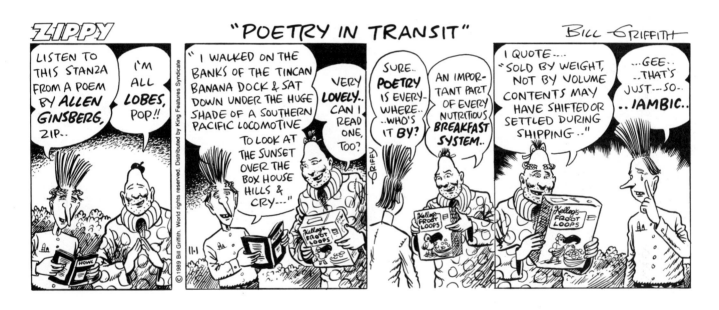

131

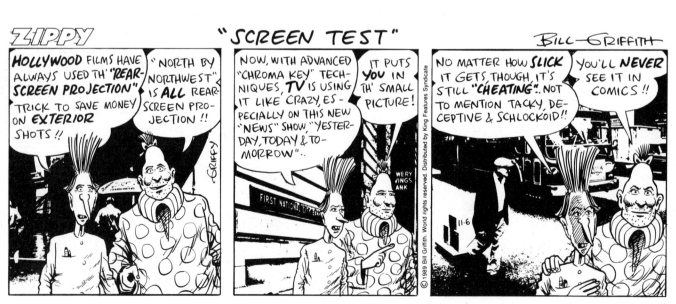

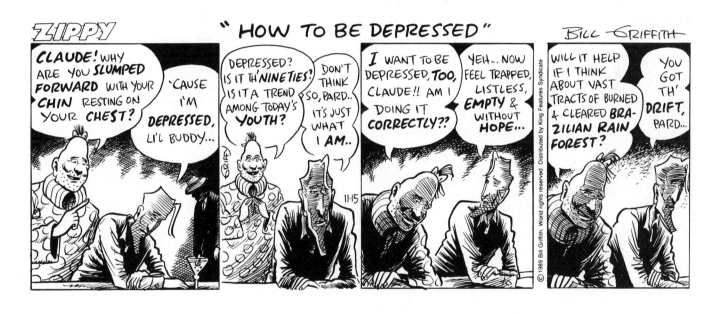

ZIPPY — "PUTTING UP A FRONT" — BILL GRIFFITH

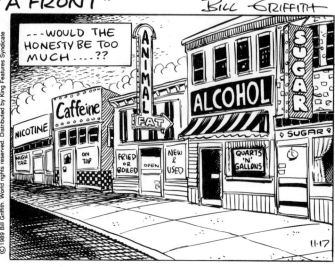

ZIPPY — "RIDING A RADIO WAVE" — BILL GRIFFITH

ZIPPY — "THE DEFINITE ARTICLE" — BILL GRIFFITH

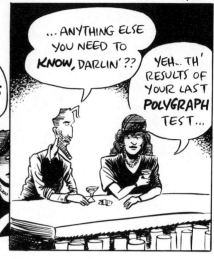

"GOT YOU COMING AND GOING"

"SEEDY PLAYER"

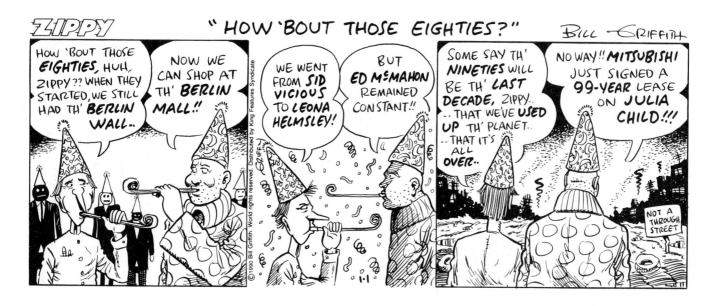

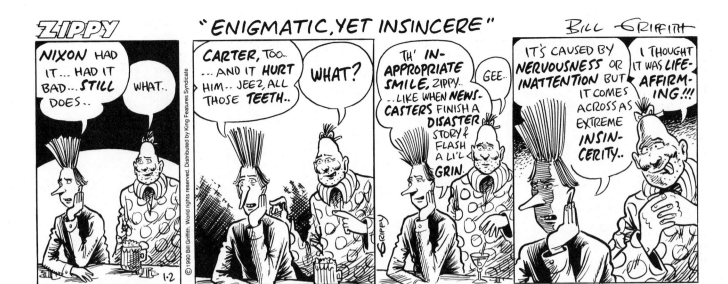

Dingy - THE MERCHANDISING EFFORT:

Dingy - THE MOVIE:

Dingy - THE BACKLASH and - THE BACKLASH TO THE BACKLASH

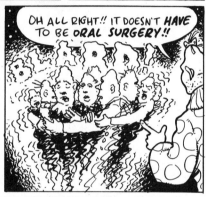

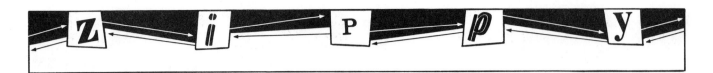

CONTINUED NEXT PAY PERIOD!!

159

ZIPPY
Planet o' the Pinheads
EPISODE 6.

THE "ADAM AND EVE LOUNGE" IN DOWNTOWN MIAMI..

..WE'RE TRYING..

NO, NO!! IT GOES IN THE OTHER END!!

FOTO-MAT HAD NO POSITIONS OPEN FOR "LIVE SEX ACTS" SO I GOT TH' "LYPPIES" JOBS IN THIS WORLD RENOWNED NIGHT CLUB!

© 1984 BILL GRIFFITH

NOW THAT I'VE PERFORMED A LIFE-ENHANCING SERVICE I THINK I'LL TREAT MYSELF TO A JAR OF FLUFFO AND 6 MONTHS OF SPACE TRAVEL!!

AHA!!

LET'S SEE.. WHERE DID I HIDE TH' SPACE-SHIP? IS IT IN THIS WAREHOUSE OR THAT WAREHOUSE?

I KNEW IT!!

ALRIGHT, PAL.. EITHER YOU TAKE ME WITH YOU OR I BLOW THE WHOLE STORY TO "REAL PEOPLE"!!

IS A MOTEL CLERK SKY-JACKING ME? OR IS THIS A SEQUENCE FROM A "CULTURE CLUB" ROCK VIDEO?

EARTH OR BUST

DO NOT TOUCH

RMMMM!

I HOPE YOU ENJOY MINGLING WITH PEOPLE FROM OTHER PLANETS!!

DON'T YOU WORRY, PAL.. SOME OF MY BEST FRIENDS ARE ALIEN LIFE FORMS!!

BLAST!!

SIX MONTHS LATER, THE DUO ARRIVES ON MICROVIA--

YOU CAN STOP DROOLING ON MY ANKLE, ASTRO-BOY... WE'RE HERE!

FLENTAVIA!! BOZ-MIROID!! WHY AREN'T YOU BODY-SURFING IN A POOL OF BLUE FOSWELD?

FOSWELD WITHDRAWL WAS JUST WHAT WE NEED-ED TO REGAIN OUR SENSE OF EMPLOYMENT OPP-ORTUNITY!!

EMPLOY-MENT? ON MICROVIA?

EOT

DRIVE THRU

YES, WE ALL OWN EITHER FOTO-MAT OUTLETS OR PIZZA-TIME FRANCHISES!! ON WEEKENDS, WE TAKE PICTURES OF MOZARELLA & INSERT SICILIAN SLICES INTO KODAK DISC CAMERAS!

..AND THE WHOLE OPERATION RUNS ON A 47% PROFIT MARGIN!

HEY, THIS IS MY KINDA ORB!!

FOTO MAT

PIZZA TIME

SALE!

PIZZA TIME

SOON...

ASK HIM ABOUT 8" BY 10" AN-CHOVIES...

..THE QUESTION IS, SHOULD WE SELL OUT TO THE JAPAN-ESE NOW OR WAIT FOR A MAXIMIZED CASH-FLOW?

BUY, SELL, BUY, SELL! DON'T BOTHER ME WITH DETAILS!!

PRESIDENT OF MICROVIA

THINK THINK THINK

ZIPPY JUST WASN'T HAVING FUN!!

YOW!! I'M BLASTING OFF FOR CINCIN-NATI !!

I MISS ANN JILLIAN'S HAIR !!

EVENTUALLY, SOME-WHERE IN OHIO--

HEY, LET'S ALL USE LOTS OF EYE-LINER, WEAR OUR BOXER SHORTS ON THE OUTSIDE AND CLIMB TO THE TOP OF THE CHARTS !!

$

RIVERFRONT

MENTAL HOSPITAL

THE END!

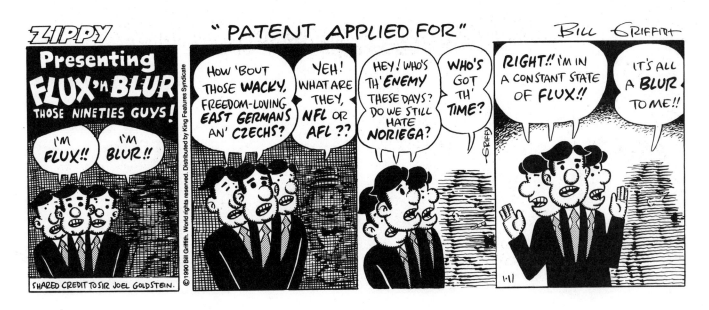

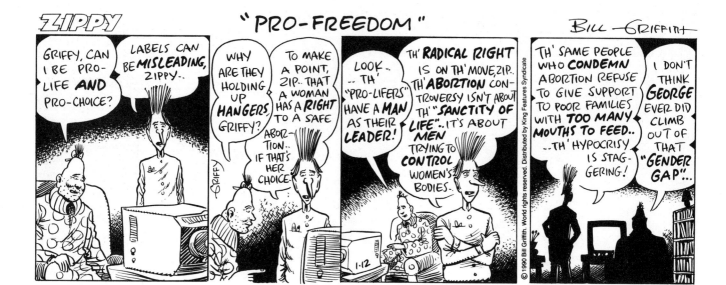

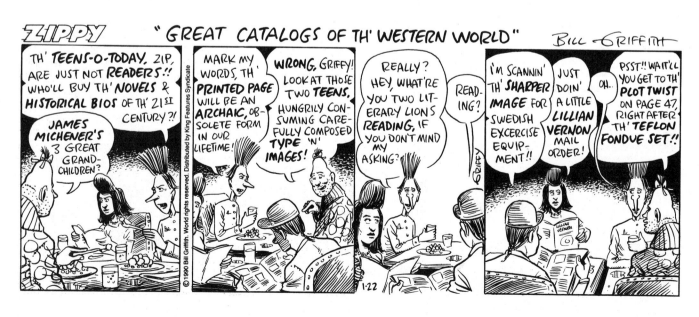

"TANKS FOR TH' MEMORIES" BILL GRIFFITH

"AND AGAIN AT ELEVEN" BILL GRIFFITH

"A REAL NEAT GUY" BILL GRIFFITH

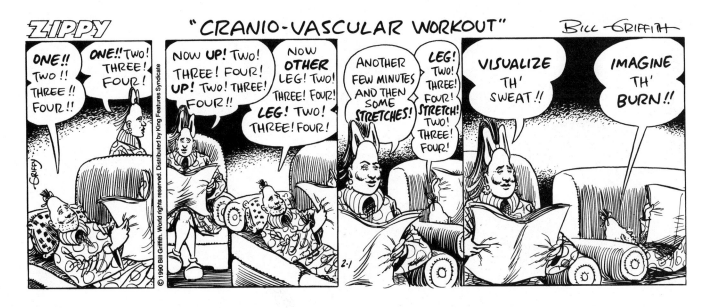

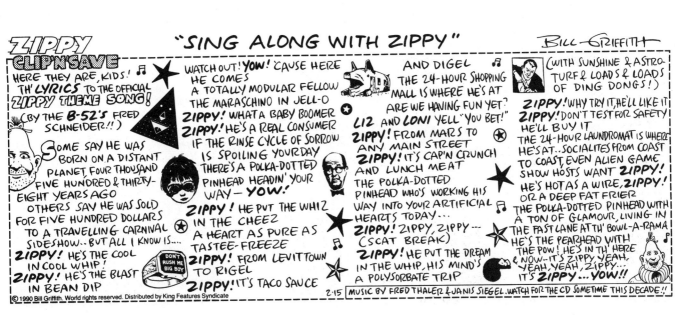

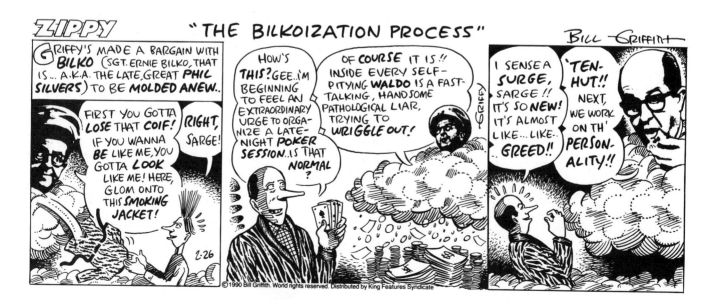

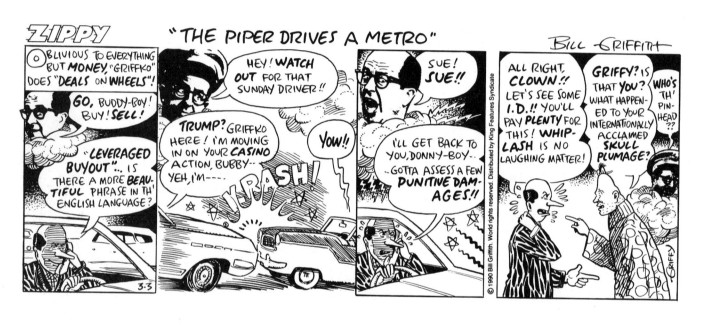

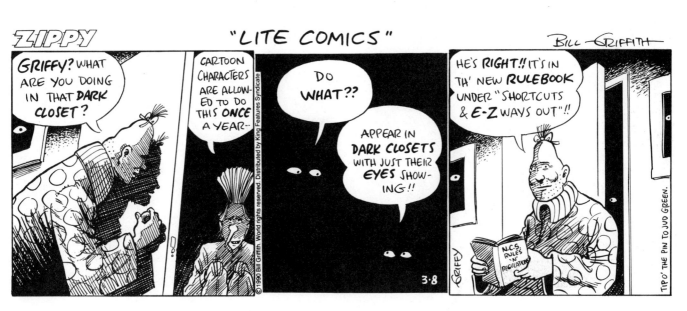

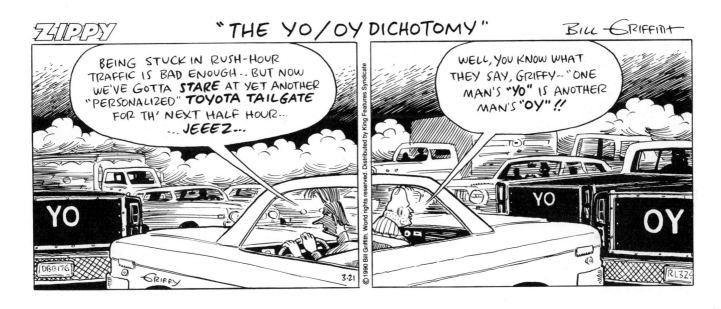

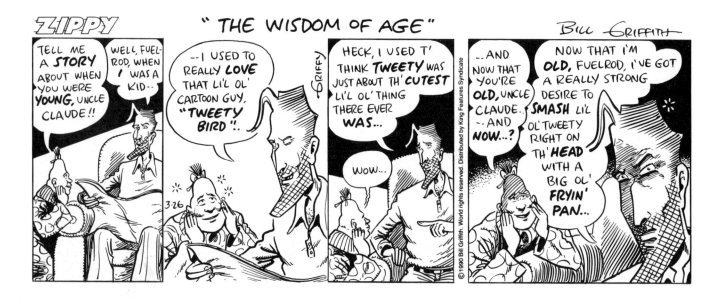

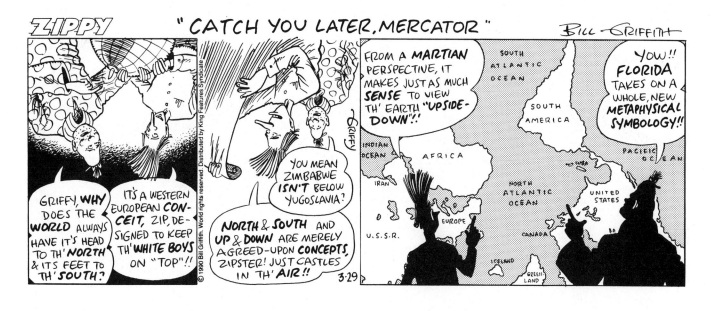

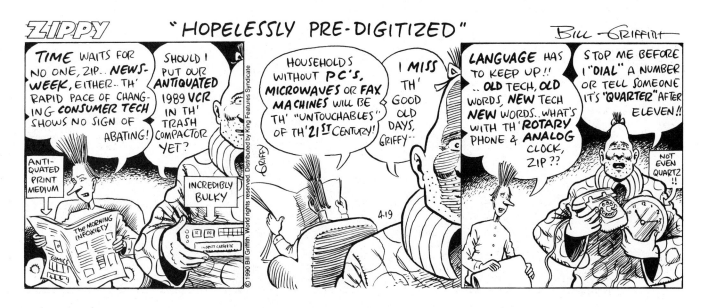

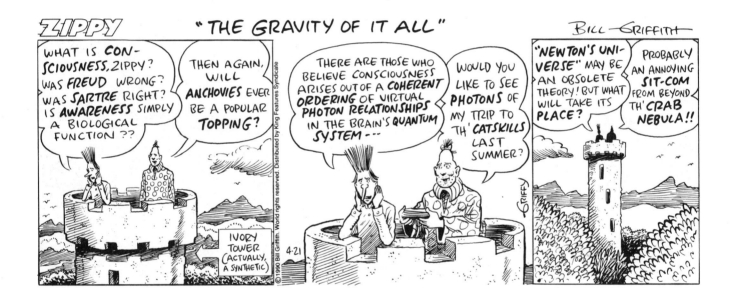

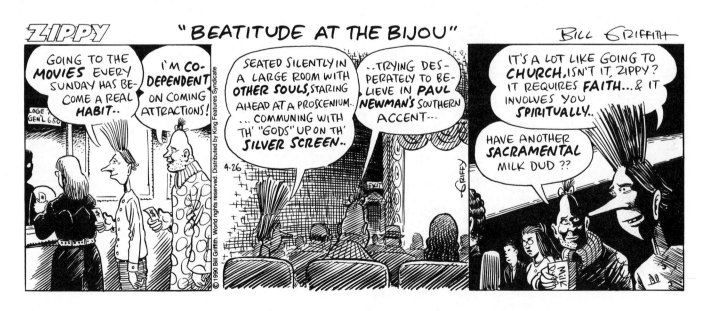

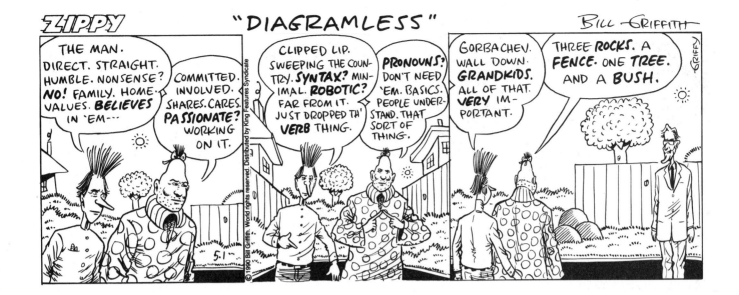

Calendar Art

Zippy calendars have been produced each year since 1982—with the exception of 1989, *The Year That Zippy Forgot.* Selected cover art and monthly drawings are featured on the following pages.

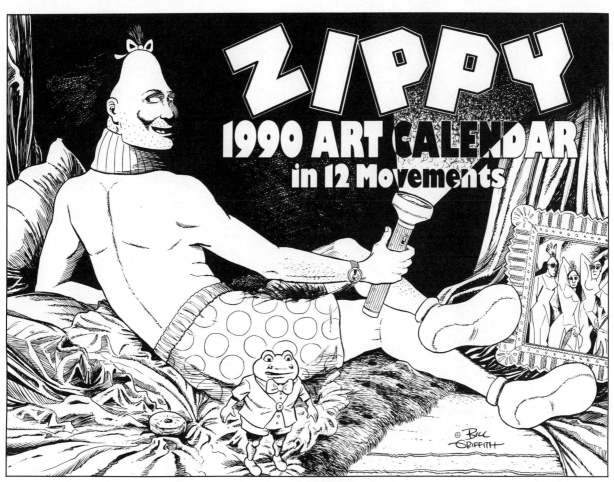

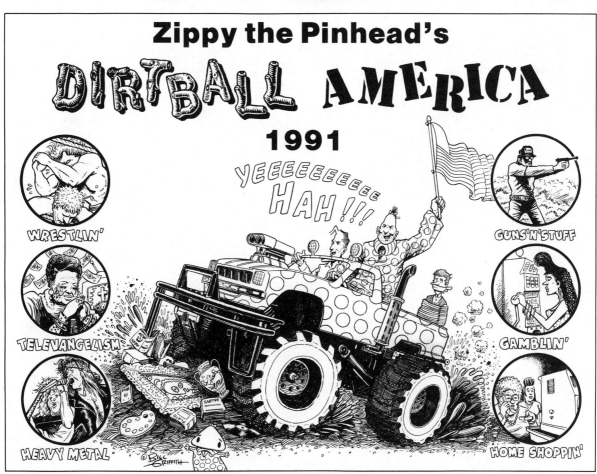

April 1982

June 1982

August 1982

September 1982.

November 1982

March 1983

January 1990

February 1990

June 1990

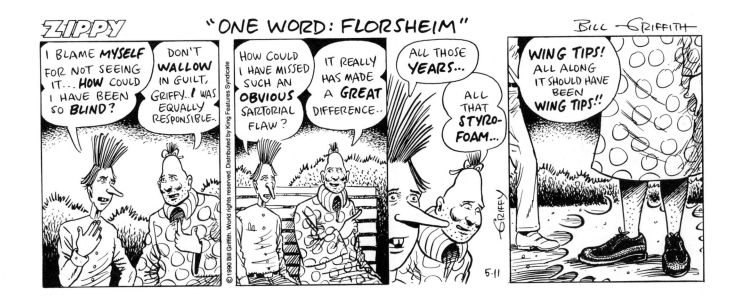

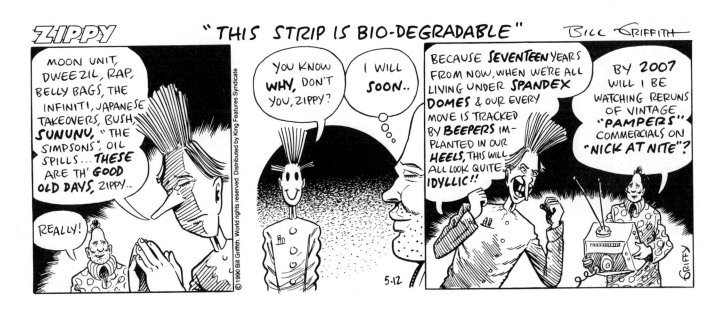

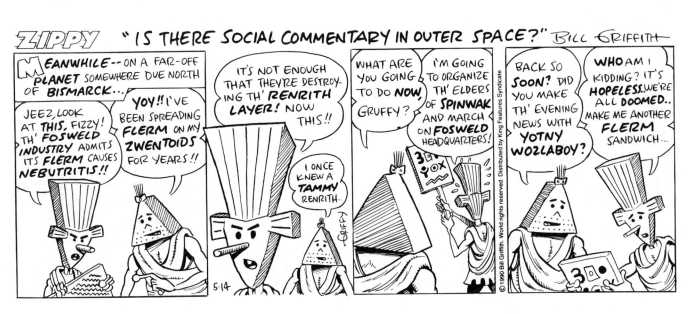

"AMPHIBIOUS VEHICLES"

BILL GRIFFITH

"HE WAS FRAMED!!"

BILL GRIFFITH

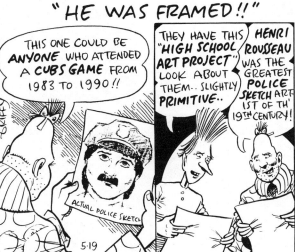

"THEME PARK"

BILL GRIFFITH

215

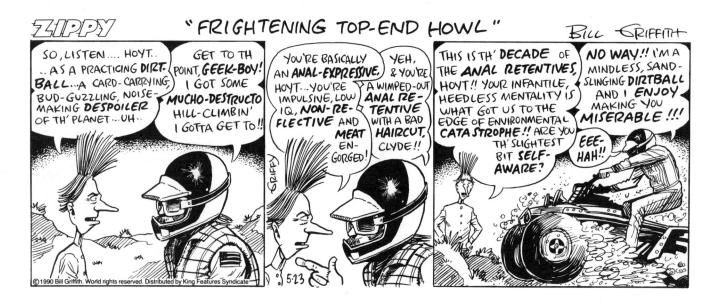

"OUT OF THE BARN & IN YOUR FACE" BILL GRIFFITH

 "THE KING THING" BILL GRIFFITH

ZIPPY **"ROCK AROUND THE BLOC?"** BILL GRIFFITH

218

"LONG DISTANCE CALL"

BILL GRIFFITH

"TOGETHER AT LAST"

BILL GRIFFITH

"ROYAL INVITATION"

BILL GRIFFITH

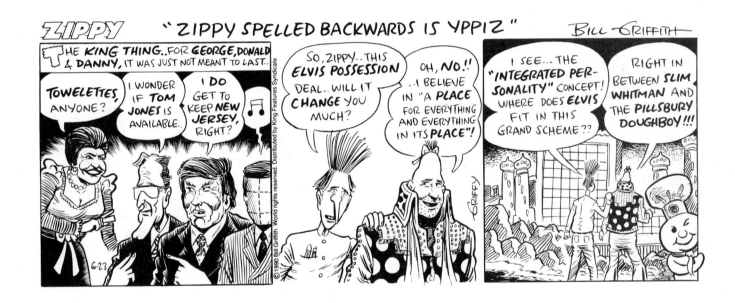

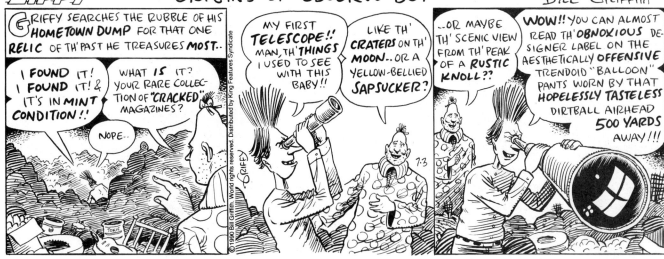

227

238

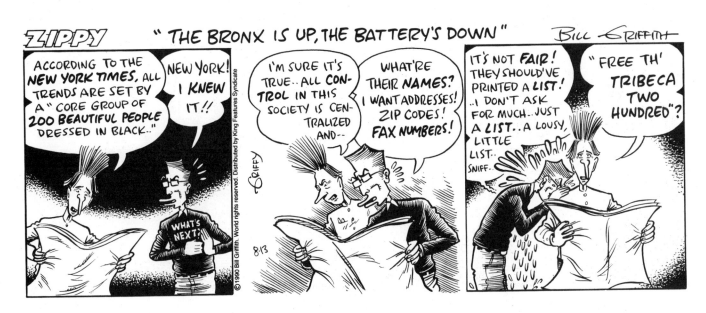

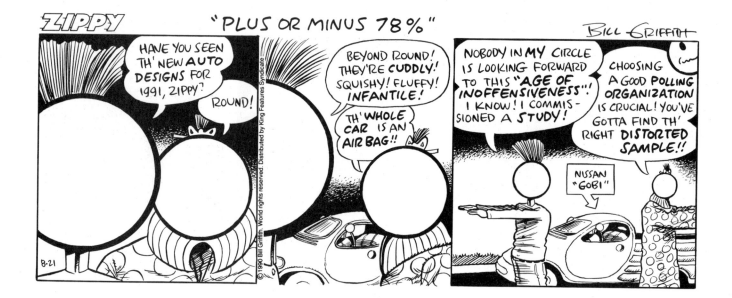

"ANALOG DIALOGUE" BILL GRIFFITH

 "CASUAL CASUALTY" BILL GRIFFITH

 "BAKED WHILE YOU SLEEP" BILL GRIFFITH

ZIPPY — "LIFE WITHOUT TOM BROKAW" — BILL GRIFFITH

INSIDE GRIFFY'S "NO NEWS IS GOOD NEWS" SANCTUARY..

I'VE CUT MYSELF OFF FROM ALL MEDIA INPUT.. ..I DON'T EVEN KNOW WHO'S IN TH' PENNANT RACE..

I DON'T KNOW ABOUT TH' LATEST OIL SPILL..OR TH' LATEST PLANE CRASH..OR TH' LATEST MIDEAST TAKEOVER..

IN MY TIMELESS, LI'L REFUGE IN TH' REDWOODS, ALL EXTRANEOUS INFORMATION HAS BEEN ELIMINATED... I'M HAVING A MENTAL ENEMA..CLEANING OUT TH' FLOTSAM & JETSAM OF... ..UH.. ..OF..

ZIPPY..?UH, LISTEN, I'M NOT LOSING MY RESOLVE OR ANYTHING.. BUT.. YOU WOULDN'T HAPPEN TO KNOW..YOU KNOW..UH..

TH' NEW FALL LINEUP ON CBS? I'VE GOT EVERY SHALLOW PREMISE COMPLETELY MEMORIZED!!

MORE TMW.!

9-21

© 1990 Bill Griffith. World rights reserved. Distributed by King Features Syndicate

ZIPPY — "SNIFF...CHOKE..GULP..." — BILL GRIFFITH

POOR GRIFFY...HE'S CONFLICTED...DOES HE OR DOESN'T HE WANT TO UNPLUG HIMSELF FROM THE SEDUCTIVE MEDIA GRID?

WAIT! NO! DON'T TELL ME!! I TAKE IT BACK! I DON'T WANT TO KNOW!!

..BUT I'VE GOT TH' LATEST ON TH' TED TURNER, JANE FONDA SIZZLER!!

NO, ZIPPY. I'VE GOTTA WORK THIS THING OUT IN PEACE.. ..I NEED TO RID MY MIND OF ALL CELEBRITY GOSSIP, FACTOIDS & DISASTER NEWS..

GEE, A COMPLETE VOID, HUH?

GOODBYE, OLD FRIEND.. ..MAYBE WE'LL MEET AGAIN SOMEDAY WHEN TH' WORLD IS A SIMPLER PLACE -- IF THAT DAY EVER COMES...

CONTINUED MONDAY!

9-22

© 1990 Bill Griffith. World rights reserved. Distributed by King Features Syndicate

ZIPPY — "THE LUCKIEST PEOPLE IN THE WORLD" — BILL GRIFFITH

ALONE AT LAST..WITHOUT TH' CONSTANT, MINDLESS CHATTER OF TH' MEDIA.. MMM!! TH' AIR IS GOOD!

I'M LIKE A DRUG ADDICT ENTERING WITHDRAWAL..IT'LL BE ROUGH, BUT I'M COMMITTED TO A THOROUGH CONSCIOUSNESS CLEANSING!

I'LL JUST TRY TO THINK ABOUT NOTHING..

Kim Basinger spotted *Batma* **Michael Keaton.** "Would you e us for one minute?" she asked, ta buss stop. "I don't get to see him o Cracked Keaton after being kissed. girl's always up for something, isn't Calling after Kim, he joked, "Are we to kiss again? Just checking." After stars ate lemon mousse and raspb while **Liza Minnelli** crooned "As

IT REALLY IS INSIDIOUS.. ..TH' WAY PEOPLE MAGAZINE HAS TOUCH TONE ACCESS TO EVERYONE'S FRONTAL LOBES---

9-24

© 1990 Bill Griffith. World rights reserved. Distributed by King Features Syndicate

ZIPPY "INFERNAL COMBUSTION" Bill Griffith

GRIFFY SITS ALONE IN TH' **REDWOODS**, TRYING TO RID HIS MIND OF TH' **INFORMATION OVERLOAD** FOISTED UPON US ALL BY TH' MEDIA'S **ENDLESS CHATTER--**

I WANT TO HEAR TH' SOUND OF **ONE CELEBRITY** FADING...

"To SEE THE WORLD IN A GRAIN OF SAND, AND HEAVEN IN A WILDFLOWER; HOLD INFINITY IN THE PALM OF YOUR HAND, AND ETERNITY IN AN HOUR..."

— WILLIAM BLAKE

9-25

?!

RRRRRRRRRRRRRR

CONTINUED TOMORROW!

ZIPPY "BAD SHOCKS" Bill Griffith

HUH? I'M **FIFTY** MILES FROM TH' NEAREST **TOWN!** AND **TWENTY** MILES FROM TH' NEAREST **ROAD!** WHAT **IS** THAT SOUND?!

RRRRRR

9-26

MY ALL-TOO-BRIEF RESPITE FROM TH' **STURM UND DRANG** OF MODERN LIFE IS **RUDELY** INTERRUPTED BY TH' **GROWL** OF A PETROLEUM-BASED **BIPED!!**

RRRRRRRRR!

IT'S PROBABLY SOME **OVERSTIMULATED** YAHOO WITH A TWISTED NEED TO **FILL** ANY **SILENCE** WITH TH' **WHINE** OF **ENGINE NOISE--**

RRRRRRRRR

YOU **CALLED, GEEK-BOY?!!**

GOD HELP US!! IT'S **HOYT** TH' **DIRTBALL!!**

MORE TMW.!

ZIPPY "IT HOYTS ALL OVER" Bill Griffith

GRIFFY'S **REDWOOD REFUGE** HAS BEEN VIOLATED BY HIS ARCH ENEMY, **HOYT THE DIRTBALL**..THESE GUYS CLASH PHILOSOPHICALLY!

TURN OFF THAT **INFERNAL COMBUSTION ENGINE,** YOU THOUGHTLESS BARBARIAN!!

HEY, THIS WAS A **DEMOCRACY,** LAST TIME I CHECKED, WIMPY! I GOT A GOD-GIVEN **RIGHT** TO MAKE NOISE!! WHOOO-EEE!!

RRRRRRRRRRRRRRR

YOU SYMBOLIZE EVERYTHING THAT'S **WRONG** WITH THIS CULTURE--YOU'RE SO **SELF-ABSORBED** YOU AREN'T EVEN **AFFECTED** BY MY **STINGING CRITICISMS!**

YOU GOT **THAT** RIGHT, DWEEB! YOUR' LI'L OL' **POINTY-HEADED** TANTRUMS JUST ROLL OFF MY **FOUR-STROKE QUAD CYCLE!**

9-27

RRRRRRRRRRRR

YOU KNOW, IT ISN'T SO MUCH A "**DUMBING DOWN**" GOING ON IN THIS COUNTRY AS A **RISE** IN **POWER** OF TH' **ALREADY DUMB!** TH' **ASCENDENCY** OF TH' **DIRTBALL!!** IT'S A NATIONAL TRAGEDY!!

WHOOO-EEE!! NOW GET OUT MY **WAY,** DOGMEAT! I GOTTA CALL IN MY **OPINION** ON TODAY'S CNN VIEWER'S POLL!!

RUM RUM RUM RUM!!